# Dr. Shivers' Carnival of Terror

## Look for these SpineChillers™

*Attack of the Killer House*
*The Venom Versus Me*
*Pizza with Extra Creeps*

# SPINE CHILLERS™

## Dr. Shivers'
## Carnival of Terror

### Fred E. Katz

THOMAS NELSON PUBLISHERS
Nashville • Atlanta • London • Vancouver

Published in Nashville, Tennessee, by Thomas Nelson, Inc., Publishers, and distributed in Canada by Word Communications, Ltd., Richmond, British Columbia. SpineChillers™ is a trademark of Thomas Nelson Publishers, Inc.

Editor: Lila Empson; Copyeditor: Nedra Lambert; Packaging: Kevin Farris Belinda Bass; Production: Brenda White, Lori Gliko.

ISBN 0-7852-7505-3

Printed in the United States of America

1 2 3 4 5 6 — 01 00 99 98 97 96

A blood-chilling scream woke me up. I jumped from the bed in my uncle's guest room and slid on the hardwood floor to the window. I couldn't believe what I saw. In the field next to my uncle's Hollywood house was a carnival. It wasn't there when I arrived yesterday from the airport. It wasn't there last night when I went to bed. Where did it and the scream come from?

I grabbed my robe and ran out of the room and down the long hallway to the stairs. As I raced down the stairs and into the family room, I heard my uncle talking in the kitchen. He was hanging up the telephone receiver when I walked through the kitchen doorway.

"Uncle Rex, where did it come from?" I asked.

"That was exactly why I was on the phone. The local police said that the carnival owners rented the field to put up their carnival. It looks like it'll be there for a few days," he told me.

"So, what do we do now, Uncle Rex?" I was hoping he'd say that I could go over and see the carnival.

Uncle Rex pretended like he was thinking really hard. "Now, let me see here, Kyle. Maybe you should wake up your traveling companions and the four of you ought to go check it out. How does that sound?"

I didn't even wait to answer him. I ran out of the kitchen and up the stairs to the other rooms to wake up my friends.

I guess I should tell you a little about myself and how I got to Hollywood from my little hometown of Carverville. My name is Kyle Conlon. My Uncle Rex called my dad and asked if I could visit over Christmas vacation. My uncle is a big-time TV producer. He produced a lot of the hits from last season. Every time he called my dad he told him about the latest big movie star he'd worked with. Uncle Rex knew a lot of Hollywood's famous people.

He was working on a new TV show and needed a few teens to screen some of the early film clips. Uncle Rex wanted "regular" kids from the Midwest. Carverville is about as Midwest as a town can get. We've got corn everywhere. And next to the corn there are cows. Yes, Carverville is the Midwest.

I asked my three best friends, Brent, Sammy, and Sara, to come along. My uncle's film studio paid for our plane tickets and sent a big black limo to pick us up at the airport. The limo had a small refrigerator, and it was filled with health food and carrot juice. Dad

2

warned me that California was different from Carverville. I began to understand what he meant after I saw the foods in the limo.

During the ride from the airport to my uncle's house Sammy was preoccupied with the buttons and gadgets in the limo. Brent looked around for movie stars. Sara and I looked at the trees and neat buildings. California didn't look anything like Carverville. The palm trees and flowering bushes made everything around us seem so fresh and beautiful. And the temperature outside was warm even though it was December. I was going to like California.

When we arrived at Uncle Rex's house, Sara's mouth dropped open. The house was bigger than any we had seen back home. The entrance hallway of the house was bigger than my parents' living room. Sammy got into trouble before our suitcases were even on the shiny marble floor.

The staircase was very long and it had a winding railing along it. The railing was perfect for sliding down. The temptation got to Sammy before I could. Suddenly, I heard a cry that sounded something like a cowboy getting wounded by a stray bullet.

"You got me, buckaroo," Sammy called out to make sure that we all noticed him.

"Sammy, don't do things like that. This isn't your house. My aunt will kill us if she catches you," I scolded.

It was too late. Aunt Janet had already walked into

the foyer. The sound of her shoes on the marble made me spin around quickly.

"That's all right, Kyle. It has been so long since kids played on that railing that I am glad to see someone using it the proper way," she said.

Sara leaned over and whispered in my ear, "This is going to be really cool. Your aunt is a neat person."

Aunt Janet continued, "Kyle, your Uncle Rex will not be home from the TV studio till later. I'll make us some dinner and then we can go swimming in the pool."

My Aunt Janet made us something to eat, showed us around the house, and led us to our bedrooms. My room was on the side of the house that overlooked an empty field next to some large warehouses.

When my aunt finally led us to the pool we were awestruck. It was the biggest pool we had ever seen. Half of the pool was inside the house and the other half was outside. A wall of glass separated the inside from the outside. We entered the pool inside the house, swam under the glass wall, and surfaced outside the house. It was cool, and definitely unlike the public pool we had in Carverville.

Uncle Rex came home while we were in the pool. My uncle was very tall and his black hair was starting to get gray. Dad sometimes kidded him about that. Uncle Rex retorted that at least he was the brother who still had hair.

It was really great to see him. He had brought home

4

a videotape of a scary movie that was going to hit the theaters in a few weeks. That impressed Sammy. We got into dry clothes and went to the family room to watch the movie on the big-screen TV.

When the movie ended it was late, and we all sleepily went off to bed. The movie must have affected my dreams. In the middle of the night I had a frightening nightmare. In it, the four of us from Carverville were trapped inside a gigantic cuckoo clock with a time bomb. The seconds ticked away, bringing us closer to the impending explosion. The scream woke me up before the bomb could explode.

I couldn't believe that my friends had slept through that scream, but they had. My room was on the side of the house next to the carnival, so I guess that's why I heard it and they didn't.

I banged on Sammy's door. "Sammy, hurry up and get out of there. You won't believe this!"

Brent and Sara heard me pound on Sammy's door, and they both walked out of their bedrooms at the same time that Sammy walked out of his. I talked rapidly, "Come on, I've got to show you something. This is really cool."

We raced into my room and pressed our faces against the window. "Uncle Rex said that this carnival rented the field next door to his house and maybe we should go check it out. Is everybody up for it?" I asked.

Sammy, Sara, and I had already turned and were heading from the room when we heard Brent scream.

When I turned around I saw a gigantic, monstrous face pressed against the bedroom window

Sara was on the floor. I thought she was having a panic attack until I listened to the noises she was making. She was laughing. I looked at the face in the window. It was a balloon that had floated up from the carnival. I had never seen one that had a monster's face painted on it.

Sammy said, "Hey, if the balloons can scare us that bad then maybe the rides can give us some good scares, too." He enjoyed being scared. To Sammy, being scared was a way to know that you were a living, breathing human being. That wasn't my favorite thing, but I had to admit that the carnival looked like a great time. Both Aunt Janet and Uncle Rex had to work that day. Going to the carnival would definitely be more exciting than hanging around the house all day with the housekeeper, even if the house did have a pool, a big-screen TV, and dozens of movies to watch.

It didn't take us more than a half hour to shower, get dressed, and make it to the breakfast table. My aunt must have anticipated our desire to get to the carnival quickly. She had already laid out sweet rolls, juice, and cereal on the table. Brent and Sammy started to eat before Sara and I even sat down. I had just poured cereal into my bowl when Aunt Janet walked into the room.

"Aunt Janet, Uncle Rex said it was okay for us to go to the carnival. Is it all right with you, too?"

A big smile spread across her face. "Sure, get over there and have a great time. If I wasn't scheduled to be in L.A. for a meeting, I would join you. It looks like a lot of fun. If you need anything, the housekeeper will be here all day."

We gulped down our food and headed for the door. Aunt Janet caught me by the arm as I was walking out. "You might need some of this. Rex left it for you before going to the studio." She handed me some money. I couldn't believe that I almost forgot money. I gave Aunt Janet a hug and then ran to catch up with the others.

I ran so fast that I didn't see that the others had stopped dead in their tracks. I slid to a halt in the gravel in front of the gate to the carnival. My three friends were staring up at the gate.

"What's up?" I asked.

Sammy pointed to the banner across the top of the gate. "Doctor Shivers' Carnival of Terror," it read. Sammy looked at me. "Awesome," he said.

"Not a very inviting name is it?" Brent gulped as he spoke.

Sammy started to walk toward the gate as he answered Brent. "This looks like a great place to spend the day. California is way cool. You would never see anything like this back in our little town."

"We've got some neat things there, too," Sara retorted.

"Like what? The last big thing that happened in Carverville was when the baptismal flooded at the church and Pastor Christensen had to wear wading boots when he gave the sermon," Sammy snapped. Just a reminder of that day made us all laugh.

"Enough, already," Brent said. "We all agree that we live in a small town and that it's a little boring sometimes. And we all agree that having a carnival next door is not an everyday experience for any of us. So let's quit the arguing and look around."

With that said, everyone stepped inside the gate except for me. I was a little uneasy about this place. After all, the carnival had been erected so quickly and mysteriously. And there was that scream that woke me up. But what really got to me was the banner on the gate. I called the other three back to me so we could talk.

"Maybe we better think this adventure through. You know, it doesn't really look like they're ready for customers. I'm thinking that it might be better if we kind of went back to the house," I said nervously.

9

Sammy gave me his you've-got-to-be-kidding look, and then he said, "Time out. Where in the world did that statement come from? You were the first one to want to come over here. I'm all excited and ready to go."

"I'm a little concerned for your safety. Remember, I invited all of you out here to California with me. If something happens to any of you, your parents will kill me. I'm not sure that an amusement park called Dr. Shivers' Carnival of Terror is safe," I argued.

Sara chimed in next. "Am I hanging out with a bunch of scaredy-cats? Let's just go in. If for some reason we get afraid of anything, we can leave. I mean what can they do, lock us in there?"

"Have a mummy chase us through a tomb?" Brent added, pointing out the silliness of my fear.

"All right. I guess I'm being a little too careful. What can it hurt?" I told them.

The four of us walked through the gate together. I was still a little unsure of the place, so I walked behind the others. My shoes had shuffled only a few steps from the gate when I was stopped by an eerie realization. Nobody else was there. No families. No kids. No workers. No one. Maybe *we* shouldn't be here either. At that moment, a wicked laugh came from behind me and a bony hand gripped my shoulder. I let out a scream.

We all spun around. I stared up into the long, sharp-featured face of a man. A thin mustache connected to a goatee gave the man's face a sinister look. On the top of his head sat a top hat like Abraham Lincoln wore. My jaw dropped open as I scanned the rest of the guy's clothing. He wore a tuxedo jacket, the kind with tails on it. It seemed very weird to me but, then again, this was California. The man's dark eyes stared down at me and my mouth went dry.

"Can I help you, my young friends?" he questioned in a slow, methodical manner. His voice sounded like he was speaking from the inside of a barrel. It sent a tingle up my spine. Even his eyes were spooky. He opened them widely at first and then squinted at me. When his eyes popped open, his eyebrows raised and then they dropped as he squinted.

Sammy jumped right in. "We're staying with Kyle's uncle. He's a TV producer and he lives next door and when we woke up and saw the carnival we thought we would be your first customers." He talked so fast that his words almost ran together.

"And that you are. But I'm afraid we're not open yet. There is still much work to be done." The man smiled at us as he spoke. "Oh, I'm sorry. I forgot to introduce myself. I am Doctor Shivers, the owner of this little traveling carnival. It is my distinct pleasure to welcome you."

I finally found my voice. "Nice to meet you, sir. When will you be open?"

"Not until tomorrow. I do hope you can come back then. I'm sure you're dying to try the carnival's amusements, games, and rides," he said, with a special emphasis on the word *dying*. I did not like how he said it. I was kind of relieved that we couldn't stay.

We started to head for the gate when he called to us. "On second thought, kids, wait a second. I have added some new rides and games. I would truly love it if you would test out my slight amusements, as we here at the carnival call our little rides and harmless games."

"Wow, yeah. That would be great. Like I said, nothing like this happens back in our little town." Sammy was nearly jumping up and down with excitement.

"Would you be so kind as to follow me back to my office and I'll give you special free admission passes that will allow you unpaid access to all of my amusements except for one, Dracula's Castle. It isn't quite finished yet. Dracula's coffin hasn't arrived from Transylvania, and it has to sit on dirt from that country. The dirt is here, and when the Transylvanians sent it, I said, 'Fangs very much.'" He laughed with eerie glee at his own joke, and then continued, "There is just so much to do in a carnival like this. So please, go ahead and enjoy yourselves as my guests, my very special guests. But I do have one request of you," he said.

Brent spoke first, "Sure. What can we do in return?"

"When you're all done, that is when you feel like you're just about dead, return to my office and tell me what you think of my little carnival of terror," the doctor said. I nodded my head that we would. I was not sure I ever wanted to see him again, but a promise was a promise.

Dr. Shivers motioned for us to follow him. We slipped between some tents and amusements. I looked at the names on the games and rides. There were some very strange things at this carnival.

His office was in a dented trailer. His picture was painted on the side, along with the words DR. SHIVERS' CARNIVAL OF TERROR. The painting was fading like it had been in the sun for a lot of years.

I opened the door and peeked inside. The room was filled with odd items. It looked like the set of a science fiction movie. A big stuffed raven stood on a perch in the corner of the office. At least, I think it was stuffed. For a moment I was sure the bird winked at me.

Dr. Shivers gave each of us a small skeleton on a

necklace. But it wasn't an ordinary skeleton. It had the face of our bizarre Dr. Shivers on the skull. He instructed us to show them at any ride or refreshment stand and we could have what we wanted for free. Sammy was right. Nothing like this would ever happen back in our hometown.

Dr. Shivers gave us one last twisted smile before we left. As we walked away from his office I heard him laugh, and something told me that everything wasn't going to be all fun and games at the carnival. I started to feel like it might indeed be filled with terror. There was definitely something sinister about that laugh.

Brent walked toward the right side of the midway, and Sammy and Sara headed down the left. I decided to join Brent. My mouth gaped. These were the strangest rides and games I had ever seen. I was sure that the others felt the same way. Friends could sense things like that.

Brent, Sammy, and Sara were my best friends. Brent and I had met a few months ago at the new church my family started going to. I liked hanging out with him and doing things together. He was a little smaller than most of the kids our age. I supposed some of the others at middle school might have picked on him except that he was a great guy. Everyone liked him. He really cared about people.

Sara's dad was the pastor of our church. I was impressed with her love of sports and her great pitching arm. Her dark brown hair was straight and hung

14

to her shoulders, but most of the time she pulled it back in a ponytail.

Sammy made life just plain fun. Everything was an adventure to him. Sammy was born in Mexico, and his family later moved to Texas. His dad was a roadway engineer and his company transferred him to a city near Carverville a couple of years ago. Sammy was the kind of guy that jumped right into whatever came along. Unfortunately, he had one drawback. He played too many practical jokes on us. A place like Dr. Shivers' Carnival of Terror was ripe for Sammy's sense of humor.

Brent and I walked by two rides that sat on top of mobile trailers. As we were looking around, Brent said, "You know, Dr. Shivers looks familiar. There was something about his eyes. He reminded me of a guy I saw on TV."

I scoffed, "Come on, Brent, a guy like Dr. Shivers would never be on TV. He's probably traveled all over the world with this carnival. Besides, if you saw him before, it was probably a picture on a 'Wanted' poster in the post office. He looked like a pretty rough character to me."

"No, he seemed okay. I know I've seen him, and if I keep thinking about it, it will all come to me," he insisted.

While we were talking someone called to us. "Hey, kids. Come on, try your luck in the Gremlins' Shooting Gallery. Three bull's-eyes and you can win a teddy bear. What do you say, kids? Give it a try. Impress your friends with your skill." The words came from a man standing in front of a shooting gallery.

I laughed and looked at Brent. "I thought this was a carnival of terror. This is like something you'd see at a carnival back home. Let's try to find something a little more exciting."

The guy yelled to us again, "Try the Gremlins' Gallery. Don't be chicken!"

"Who's a chicken?" said a voice from behind us. I spun around and Sammy and Sara were standing there. "We're not chickens. What's there to be afraid of in a shooting gallery?" Sara responded.

"I'm sorry, kids. I thought I was talking to a gang of middle schoolers. Maybe this might be too frightening for all of you," the man by the gallery taunted Sara.

"I'm going in. Anybody joining me?" Sara called as she walked forward. We all fell in line behind her.

"Just follow the stairs up to the gallery and walk down the hall, folks," the guy instructed as we entered.

The stairway got darker as we neared the top. When we reached the hall the others started goofing around, and I moved to the front of the line. I bumped into a wall at the end of the hallway, then Sammy bumped into me, and Brent and Sara bumped into Sammy.

Sammy yelled, "Hey, this hallway ended. Where do we go now?"

"If it doesn't go anywhere then maybe we need to

turn around and go back," Sara suggested. She had barely gotten the words out of her mouth when a panel slid across the hallway sealing us inside.

"Hey, what is this? What's happening? I can't see a thing," I yelled.

"Attention please, welcome to the Gremlins' Shooting Gallery. In a moment the wall before you will open, and you will have three seconds to seek cover before the gremlins begin shooting. And remember, if they hit three of you, you win a teddy bear . . . that is, if you live to collect your prize." The voice came from a speaker above us.

"I'm scared, Kyle," Brent whispered.

"It's a joke. It's got to be a joke. Don't you think, Sammy?" I questioned.

"Of course it is," Sammy said fearlessly.

When Sammy finished his statement, the wall slid open. This was no joke after all. Before us was a group of large wooden ducks, and on the other side of the shooting gallery counter stood a bunch of gremlins. Their beady eyes peered through the scopes on their rifles. They were cackling.

The voice from the speaker screamed with urgency, "Your three seconds are up. Take cover!"

I heard the bang from a rifle and there was an explosion behind me. The wood splintered and a piece struck me. Another shot rang out, then another. I dove behind one of the ducks. Sammy and Sara were right behind me. In the dim light I could see them crouching to take cover. Then Brent screamed.

"I've been hit!"

I spun around when I heard Brent's scream. I saw a scratch on his forearm. He was in shock and stood still like a statue. I yelled to him to get down—and fast.

I dove from behind the large wooden duck and slid to a spot at Brent's feet. I regained my footing and grabbed him by the waist, pulling him down. He fell next to me. The quick fall reminded him of where we were.

"How do we get out of here?" he whispered.

"I don't know. I think the doors have sealed us in. Sammy, Sara, are you all right?" I called to them.

"What's going on? This is crazy," Sara yelled back over the sound of the rifle shots.

"Sara, crawl back toward the wall and see if you can get the doors open. Be careful though, and stay down," I told her.

Sammy spoke next, "Brent, are you okay?"

"I'm fine. It's just a scratch."

"I see a splinter in his arm. He was nicked by a

splinter of wood when the bullet hit the wall," I added. "Sara, did you find anything yet?"

"Nothing. This door is sealed off tight. Try the wall by you and I'll try the one by me."

As long as we stayed low or behind the wooden ducks we were safe. The gremlins were just tall enough to reach the rifles. They couldn't aim their rifles downward unless they were on the counter separating us. I crawled low to the ground all the way to the side wall. I pushed and kicked the wall. I even rubbed it. Nothing. There wasn't even a seam dividing the pieces of wood. We were sealed inside.

I kicked the wall again, and then a bullet hit just above my head. I went flat to the floor and spun my head around. The gremlins had figured it out. They were crawling onto the counter.

"Kyle, get back behind the ducks. The gremlins are on the counter. They could nail you. Sara, do the same thing," Sammy yelled to us.

"Heading back now," Sara responded as she took a headlong dive toward the duck. She landed next to Sammy. I saw what she did and imitated it. Sara and Sammy were behind one duck and Brent and I were behind another. We were stuck. There didn't appear to be a way out.

"What now? Any ideas?" I asked.

"What we need now are prayers. Anybody up for an old-fashioned prayer meeting?" Sammy joked to relieve our fear and tension. I figured even he had to be scared now.

But I didn't have time to feel any relief because the next bullet exploded on the floor next to my foot. I rolled over again and took a peek. Other gremlins were joining the ones already on the counter. The situation was getting worse.

"We haven't got much time left. The gremlins are starting to cover the counter. They'll be able to hit us if we aren't behind the ducks," I said.

"Sammy, how many gremlins are on the counter now?" Sara asked.

Sammy carefully peeked around the corner of the duck. The moment his eyes moved to the edge of the duck, explosions hit the wall behind him. "I didn't have time to count but it must be all of them, and I think they've sent out for more friends."

"I wish they'd send out for pizza and leave us alone." Brent crossed his arms over his chest and sank deeper behind the duck as he spoke.

"We'll get out, Brent," Sammy encouraged. "It may not be through a door, but we'll find a way. Remember this is only a carnival. I'm sure Dr. Shivers has no intention of killing all his customers. That would really be bad for business."

"Sammy's right," Sara added. "In fact, I have total confidence that this is simply an amusement. Nobody would try to kill their customers. Would they?"

21

"It isn't good for customer loyalty," Brent chirped in.

A barrage of explosions popped all around us. We huddled closer to the center of the ducks.

"I have total confidence that our first amusement may be our last one, forever," I said.

Just then I heard the sound of padded, clawed feet hitting the floor. The gremlins were jumping off the counter. They wanted better shots. Not even the ducks could protect us now.

I heard the gremlins moving toward us. I held my breath. I really wished I could see my family and my dog one more time. I wished Uncle Rex would have told us to stay home. I wished a lot of things, but most of all I wished we could get out of this place.

"Do you hear that?" Brent whispered to me.

"The gremlins," I answered.

"No, that humming noise. I can feel a vibration underneath the floor. What's going on?" Brent added.

The floor moved. It started to tilt. I tried to hold on to a duck, but the floor's tilt increased by the second. Soon Sammy and Sara banged into Brent and me, and the four of us slid toward the wall. We were going to smack into it. And I was the one nearest the wall.

The gremlins were screaming behind us. Their section of the floor hadn't tilted. I saw them jumping up and down in frustration. The four of us slid closer to the wall. In a few seconds we would crash into it.

We hit the wall and passed through it. When the

floor tilted it exposed a black plastic wall that wasn't attached at the bottom. We slid out into the daylight and fell on air mattresses next to the amusement's side wall.

"That was great!" Sammy yelled. "This place is fantastic. What do we do next?"

"Next? I think we ought to get out of here," I said. "We could have been killed in there."

"Come on, it was just a game. I mean, we got out of there, right? Besides, we just got here. This place could be a lot of fun. Let's try another one, just to see."

"Sammy's right. Let's try something else. What else do we have to do? And don't forget that Dr. Shivers is counting on us to give him some feedback," Brent said.

Sammy was already headed for the Shoot the Chute. It was a very tall structure that had a series of inflated plastic tubes that branched off the center. The whole thing looked like a really tall spider with a dozen legs. The tubes ran all over the place. Some to the front, some to the back, and a few even stretched to other parts of the carnival. I had to admit it looked like fun.

A long stairway led to the top. We ran up the first twenty steps. Brent and I got winded so we took the next stairs a little slower. I was panting by the time I reached the top. I collapsed next to Brent, who had already sat down to catch his breath.

Sammy and Sara stood on the platform in the midst

of all the inflated tubes. They scanned the tubes, trying to decide which ones they would choose.

Sammy spoke first. "Sara, this is great. Hey, Kyle and Brent, each tube has a name on it. This one is The Devil's Doorway, and this one is The Twister."

"Do they have one called Tube to Oblivion? That's where I'm going if I can ever stand up again. My legs feel like rubber," I joked.

Sara said seriously, "That's why I'm choosing the longest tube I can find. I want to get off my aching feet for the next few minutes." With that statement, Sara moved to a tube, sat down inside, and started to slide. We could hear her yelling, "This is fantastic," the whole way down.

Sammy picked The Twister and hopped in. He hollered, "Yabba dabba doo," as he slid down. Sammy was a product of way too much TV as a young boy.

"I'm taking The Lizard's Leap," Brent said. He dropped out of sight.

I was glad that the others had already gone down. I didn't want anyone to see me when I plopped my legs inside the tube marked, Soft and Smooshy. It sounded like something for little kids. That was okay with me. All I wanted was a rest and no weird twists and turns.

I slid down, then shot upward, and then downward again. A few times I bounced off the rubbery plastic sides and spun around in the tube. This was fun! I wished now that I had taken one of the other tubes so the ride would have lasted longer. I was really enjoying myself. At least, that's what I thought until my tube ride ended.

I expected to land on the ground outside the Shoot the Chute. Instead, I dropped a few feet into a spongy, soft, slippery, gooey mess. The more I struggled to get out, the deeper I sank. I was inside something, but I didn't know what that something was. It was pitch black. What now? I started to yell for help.

At the exact moment I yelled, something crashed into the goo next to me. I heard it thud, then thrash around. Whatever it was, it fell too close for my comfort.

I screamed. It screamed back.

"Sara, is that you?" I asked with great relief.

"Kyle, it's me. But where are we?" I could tell from her voice that she was shaken up by her abrupt arrival.

"I don't know, but if you keep moving around in this stuff, you'll sink both of us. Stand still for a second," I told her. Each time she moved I could feel her sinking deeper. When she grabbed on to me, I started to sink farther down as well. We had to get out.

"Kyle, have you tried calling for help?" Sara asked.

"I only got here a few seconds before you." I answered her while I was trying to figure a way out of this. "Sara, we need to do this slowly. Walk in any direction until we reach the wall. We must be inside the Shoot the Chute. There has got to be a wall at the edge. Maybe we can punch through it or go under it."

We both started to move in opposite directions. It was hard pushing my body through the goo. It didn't seem wet, but my feet and legs worked very hard with each step. I made a mental note not to tell our gym teacher, Ms. Megamuscle Moreno, because she'd install one of these pits at the middle school.

"Kyle, I reached the wall," Sara said.

"Good, I think I'm almost there, too," I called back.

"I'm touching the wall now. I feel a rope," she said.

"Don't pu—"

"I'm pulling it," she yelled to me.

I was too late. She had already pulled it. At Dr. Shivers' Carnival of Terror you didn't want to do anything that could make things worse. A gremlin could drop through one of those tubes next. It was too late to warn her.

"What's that sound, Kyle?"

We heard a hissing. It was like air escaping from a bike tire, only it sounded like a tire from one of those monster pickup trucks.

I screamed to Sara, "Quick, make it to the middle. This place is starting to deflate. We'll be crushed by the walls."

I heard Sara huffing and groaning as she sloshed through the goo to the center. I moved toward her sounds and she moved toward mine. The hissing grew louder. I could almost feel the heavy plastic sagging around us.

Then it collapsed. I closed my eyes and waited for the end.

I heard laughing.

I opened my eyes and saw that the Shoot the Chute

had collapsed all around us and we were standing in the warm California sun again. Sammy and Brent were laughing at us.

"What are you guys laughing at?" Sara asked.

"You two," Sammy said. "How did you get in there and why were your eyes closed? You looked like you expected the world to come to an end."

"Close enough. Help us out of here," I responded.

"Does anybody else think we should leave this place?" Sara asked.

"Just because you two had a bad experience doesn't mean we should leave. Why don't we just go on something nice and easy. How about the merry-go-round? If you two are scared, then maybe a kiddy ride will be just the ticket," Sammy mocked as he helped pull Sara and me out of the goo.

Sammy was right. We should not rush out. It could have been that we got two very odd and unusual amusements. We climbed out and headed toward the merry-go-round.

Brent was the first one on. He seemed really happy to find a ride that couldn't hurt us, scratch us, or dump us in some goo. Sammy bounded onto the biggest horse he could find. Sara and I climbed onto the two smaller horses between Sammy's and Brent's. After we all sat down the merry-go-round started slowly. I didn't see an operator, but that didn't surprise me. Everything at Dr. Shivers' carnival was a little strange.

"Hey look, a brass ring," Sammy called to us.

He was trying to reach it. It was too far away from me, so I didn't try. On the third time around, I read the sign over it. It said, DON'T PULL THE BRASS RING.

I yelled to Sammy, "The sign says 'Don't pull the—' "

But it was too late. His finger slipped inside the ring and grabbed it. Out it came.

"I got it!" he said triumphantly.

I readied myself to tell him what the sign said, and that he was crazy for doing that, when the merry-go-round started to speed up. Sammy thought it was great fun, but saw terror and fear on Brent's face. Each second it spun faster and faster.

I started to climb off my horse and reach for Brent, when the wooden pony bucked me. I grabbed for the neck of the horse and held on. Soon all the horses were bucking.

"Hold on, we're in for a wild ride," Sara said.

Our horses bucked up and down as the carousel spun faster and faster. I was getting dizzy and could barely hold on.

I gripped the horse's neck tighter, but each time it bucked it loosened my grip. I went a few inches into the air. I noticed some letters were branded into the leather rein of my horse. The bucking made it hard to read them.

PULL— I read, but the horse bucked me into the air before I could finish reading.

PULL BACK— I read when I landed back on the horse. Then another buck sent me a few inches higher. The merry-go-round was spinning faster. I didn't have much time.

PULL BACK ON THE— I noticed Sara was slipping off her horse. The centrifugal force of the spinning carousel would soon throw her into the midway.

PULL BACK ON THE REINS— The wooden animal tossed me a few inches higher that time.

PULL BACK ON THE REINS HARD— I needed to stay seated long enough to read all the words, but the up-and-down motion and the spinning made it very difficult. Sammy was still smiling and yelling.

PULL BACK ON THE REINS HARD TO— To what? What happens when I pull back hard on the reins? I've got to find out. The next buck of the horse dropped me hard. I slipped to the side of the horse. I struggled back into the saddle just before the next toss hit me. This time I had to hold on and read the letters.

PULL BACK ON THE REINS HARD TO STOP, it read.

"Everybody, pull back hard on your reins. It will stop the merry-go-round," I yelled. They did as I said. The carousel started to slow. The bucking stopped, and soon the merry-go-round came to a halt.

I let out a long sigh. Brent and Sara did the same, but Sammy had jumped down from his horse and was running into the midway. He looked at us and motioned for us to follow him. "What do we go on next?" he asked. The three of us staggered off the carousel with our heads spinning from the wild ride.

"Next, we go home," Brent shot back.

"Come on, there's nothing like this back in our little town," Sammy was pleading. "Let's try something else. Look, there's a Ferris wheel. We'll go on it. We'll get high enough to look down on the whole carnival. Then we'll pick out a couple of safe-looking rides that Dr. Shivers can't turn into something that will give you a heart attack. How about it?"

"Okay, but if we don't see anything then that's it. We go back to Kyle's uncle's house." Brent was insistent.

We staggered to the Ferris wheel and jammed ourselves in the bucket. After I sat down I looked up. I shouldn't have, because every time I saw a sign around this place it scared me. This one read, THE FEAR-US WHEEL.

"This isn't a Ferris wheel," I said. My three friends stared back at me like I had lost some of my brains on the merry-go-round. "Look, the good doctor calls this a Fear-Us Wheel. I think we should get out before something crazy happens on this thing."

I spoke too late. The safety bar snapped down on us, making it impossible to get out. A glass enclosure moved down across the front and sides of the bucket. We started to move.

At first it was just the slow, usual circular movements of a Ferris wheel. The others made fun of my fearful attitude. We looked out of the glass for neat rides and amusements we wanted to go on.

I still didn't trust this place. I wished my aunt or uncle would come get us for some reason. Any reason would be good. I didn't want my friends to think I was chicken, but if the truth be told, I was scared—very scared.

The Fear-Us Wheel bucket was rounding the top when it stopped. "I warned you guys, but nobody ever listens to me," I mumbled, using my best I-told-you-so voice.

"It'll start again. Someone else must be getting on," Sara said hopefully.

"Like who? The Munsters?" I scoffed.

The Fear-Us Wheel swayed from side to side. My stomach was getting upset. I think I discovered what seasickness felt like.

"What do we do now?" Brent asked.

"Wait. All we can do is wait and see what Dr. Shivers has up his sleeve," Sara answered.

"Spiders," Sammy said.

"Dr. Shivers has spiders up his sleeve?" Sara was puzzled.

"No, there are spiders on our Fear-Us Wheel bucket." He said it like he was giving the answer to a teacher's question. He was very calm. Brent wasn't.

"Don't say that. I am really afraid of spiders. I mean deathly afraid of spiders." Brent covered his eyes with his hands as he spoke.

"Brent, he's not kidding. There are spiders on the outside of the glass. But in here we should be safe from them. Besides, with four of us here we should be able to handle a handful of spiders." As I said that more and more began to crawl onto the outside of the glass. In a couple of minutes the glass was covered with spiders, hundreds of them.

Brent opened his eyes and saw them. I thought he was going to climb out of the bucket and jump from it. Sara and I held him down.

"Don't look," Sara warned him.

"What do you mean, don't look. I'm in a nest of spiders and you tell me not to look! I want to see what is going to wrap me in its web and come back to devour me! I'm going to be spider stew! Who is going to explain to my mother that I was a snack for a bunch of spiders? Someone get us out of here!" he yelled.

We all started to scream for help. The bucket rocked back and forth. We swayed from side to side. I hoped the movement would shake off the spiders. It didn't affect them at all. They continued to crawl all over the glass. I was surprised that none got inside the bucket.

The swaying stopped. The Fear-Us Wheel began to move again. It slowly descended to the bottom. We stopped with a jolt, the safety bar flew up, the glass slid back, and we bolted from the bucket.

"Keep the spiders away from me," Brent said.

I looked back at the bucket. There wasn't a spider anywhere. Not on the ground, not on the bucket, and not on the glass. That was weird—very weird.

"What now?" Sammy was still optimistic that this place was great.

"I'm up for leaving," Sara said.

"Hey, let's win a stuffed animal before we go," Sammy pleaded.

It seemed like a reasonable request. Maybe it would help us forget the spiders. And besides, everything had turned out okay, so far.

Sammy was the first one to the game booth. "All we've got to do is hit one of those two black dots sticking up from behind that board. It looks easy enough. Look, there are three balls."

"You three go ahead," Brent said. "I need some time out. Spiders make me a little weak in the knees."

Sammy grabbed the first ball, wound up, and let the ball fly. It missed by a foot. He shrugged his shoulders and moved out of the way.

I took the next try. Baseball wasn't really my sport, and pitching was what I was the worst at. I probably would have done better if I closed my eyes. At least I wouldn't have seen the ball miss the target by three feet. I did hit one of the stuffed animals on the shelf behind the targets.

"Do I get to keep what I hit?" I joked. I thought it was pretty funny, but the others just scoffed.

"My turn," Sara said as she grabbed the ball. Sara was our last chance at winning. She was also our best chance. She pitched for our Little League team. Last year she even threw a no-hitter. She rubbed the ball and eyed the target. Sara wound up, and the pitch was good. It struck the target right in the center of the black spot.

"You did it!" Brent yelled.

"I knew you could, Sara. All those tips I gave you really worked," Sammy kidded.

"They're moving," I said nervously.

"What's moving, Kyle?" Sara asked.

"The black spots are moving. Look—they're starting to get higher." I pointed at the targets, and we saw two long antennae rise over the shelf. They were attached to a greenish, fish-scaled head. Long, jagged teeth appeared when the beast roared at us.

"Those weren't targets. They were eyes. And it is really mad!" Sammy yelled.

37

"Run for it," Brent yelled.

We turned around as the door to the carnival game was sliding shut. *Not again*, I thought. Sammy dove out and Sara was only inches behind him. I pushed Brent as the sliding doors got closer and closer.

Sara saw a pole leaning against the outside wall of the ball-toss game. She grabbed it and wedged the pole between the sliding doors. It stopped them, and she and Sammy pulled Brent through.

I dove for the opening. I had just cleared it when a slimy hand grabbed my leg. I felt the scales and the claws wrap tight around my calf.

"It's got me. I can't get out," I yelled. I figured that I was going to be this green sea monster's mid-morning snack. I tried kicking his hand away, but this refugee from the sea was too strong.

Sammy jumped up to see what he could do. His head bumped the pole holding the doors open and knocked it loose. The doors continued their slide together until they closed on the monster's arm. I heard it moan and then it let go of me.

This place was weirder than I imagined. I lay on the ground breathing a sigh of relief when something moved between me and the sun. It was a shadow. I turned my head in the dirt to see what it was.

A clown stood over us. He honked his horn. I think he was saying hello. Everybody turned when they heard the horn.

"Hey, it's a clown," exclaimed Sara.

"Brilliant deduction, Sherlock," Sammy mocked.

"Maybe he can tell us about this place. Mr. Clown, sir, we've run into some very weird stuff around here. What's behind all this?" Brent asked.

He didn't answer. He reached deep into his pants pocket and pulled out a coin. He held it in one hand and then grabbed it with the other. The clown waved the empty open hand over the closed one with the coin in it, beeped his horn, and then opened his hand. The coin was gone.

He walked over to me, reached behind my ear, and took out the coin. He never said a word.

Sara looked puzzled. She turned to us and said, "I think he was trying to tell us something. The trick means something."

"Oh, good, we're all going to disappear and then reappear in Kyle's ear. That's comforting." Sammy laughed as he spoke.

"Let me ask him another question." Sara turned

again to the clown. "Are you an important person at the carnival?"

"Why ask him something stupid like that? He's just a clown," Sammy tossed in.

The clown ignored Sammy's comment and reached into his pocket again. He pulled out a large red cloth with his left hand and draped it over his right hand. He held his right hand out in front of him with his palm up. He passed his left hand over the cloth three times, beeped his horn, and grabbed the cloth. When he lifted it, a flower appeared in a pot.

We applauded.

Sammy turned to Sara and asked, "Okay, so what does a flower have to do with his being important?"

"I get it," Brent said. "The flower was a forget-me-not. I guess we shouldn't forget him."

"I think it will be hard to forget anything around this place. I've got a question for him. Are we in danger here? What will happen if we stay?" I asked the clown.

He pulled a rope from his baggy pants and tied several knots in it. He then held it up for us to see. It was a hangman's noose. I grabbed Sara, she grabbed Brent, and Brent grabbed Sammy.

That was all I needed to see. I turned and took off. The other three were right behind me. We didn't know where we were going. We just ran. After a few minutes, I looked back and noticed that the clown wasn't following us.

I skidded to a stop. "He's not behind us. We can stop now. Does that answer everyone's questions? We need to get out of here or this will turn out to be the end of the road for us," I said.

"All right by me," Brent concurred.

"I want something to eat first," Sammy said. Every time we were ready to leave, Sammy had one more reason to stay.

We walked to a refreshment stand. Inside the stand, an older woman gave us a big smile and said, "Can I get you kids something?"

Sammy was up to the window first. "Sure, I want a hot dog."

She grabbed one from the shelf behind her. It was

wrapped in a foil wrapper and was already prepared for someone to eat it.

"I'm glad to get rid of this stuff. Dr. Shivers had me test out some of the new equipment, and this food would have been tossed out. So go ahead and have that hot dog on the house," the vendor said with a big smile. "And what can I get you?"

"Cotton candy, please," Brent responded. Neither Sara nor I wanted anything.

The woman was very kind. Her smile gave me hope that Dr. Shivers' Carnival of Terror was not all bad. As we turned to walk away, the woman closed the refreshment stand and headed the other way.

Sammy bit into his hot dog and it barked. We all turned and looked at him.

"It wasn't me," he said. "My hot dog barked."

"Sure it did," Sara scoffed.

"It did. Listen." He bit into the hot dog again. It barked. Sara started laughing. Sammy then caught the giggles, and when he laughs it doesn't take long until he's on the ground. I was walking over to look at the hot dog when I heard Brent scream.

"There are worms in my cotton candy! My cotton candy is filled with worms!" He dropped it on the ground.

# 11

Brent hopped up and down, shaking his hands in the air. The worms really grossed him out. Sara and I nearly bumped heads reaching down to pick up the cotton candy. Sammy was still laughing. His barking hot dog had struck him so funny that he couldn't stop. Sara grabbed the cotton candy first, scooped it up, and looked inside. It freaked her out, too, and she dropped it.

"Come on, I wanted to see it, too," I said in frustration. This carnival kept getting weirder by the minute.

Sara gagged and turned her head away from the pink, spun sugar. "You don't want to see it."

"I do," I snapped. I grabbed the paper cone with the cotton candy around it from the bottommost tip. I didn't want to get the worms all over me. When I tipped it over and looked inside, I saw them creeping and crawling inside the paper cone. It was gross.

I looked at Brent. "Did you eat any of it?"

"Yes," he gagged out.

43

Sammy was still laughing as he spoke, "At least you got some protein with every bite."

"That's not funny, Sammy," Brent shot back.

"Hold it, now. We can't get mad at one another. We're supposed to be having fun here," I said as I moved between the two.

"If you think eating worms is fun, then I'm having a ball," Brent said, and then he broke out in giggles. He realized how ridiculous our conversation had become. My laughter followed. At first I only giggled, then it grew into full-fledged belly laughs.

Sammy stopped laughing long enough to stand up to see the cotton candy. But when he looked at it he burst into laughter again, falling to the ground and holding his stomach. "Somebody stop me. It hurts."

Sara alternated between gagging and giggling until she caught the laughing bug as well. When Sara laughed she threw her head back in the air and let out the funniest and loudest laughs I ever heard.

"My hot dog barked," Sammy howled from the ground.

"And I had the cotton candy that ate Hollywood," Brent snorted out.

The laughter relieved our tension over Dr. Shivers' carnival. We sat up and then crawled to our feet. Sammy was still on the ground and Sara reached her hand down to help him up. Sara looked at him and asked, "Don't you think there's a lot of weird stuff around here?"

"This could all be a dream," Sammy said.

"If this is a dream," I answered, "then someone pinch me."

No one pinched me.

We started to walk down the midway, looking at all the amusements and talking about the strange events. None of us could explain why all this was going on. As far as we knew, Dr. Shivers had put together one very frightening carnival. It was really living up to its name, the Carnival of Terror.

"It all seems a little fishy to me," Sara said. "I mean, think about it. Gremlins? Sea monsters? Barking hot dogs? These things can't be real, right?"

Sammy butted in, "And why did the spiders disappear when we got off the Fear-Us Wheel? I agree, there's something fishy going on."

"Then what do we do?" I was ready for some answers.

Sara looked at me and said, "I say that we stay here and figure out what's behind the Carnival of Terror."

"Great," Sammy added, "then let's hit another ride." He looked around, but by the time we stopped talking we had reached the end of the midway. "Nothing's here. Let's head back the other way."

Brent stood at the front of the tent at the end of the midway. "The sign says the next show is in two minutes. I could use a few minutes to sit down."

Sara and I shrugged our shoulders as if to say, "That's okay by us." I thought to myself, *It isn't a ride, a shooting gallery, or even food. So it must be fine.* Sammy didn't want to see the show. He wanted to go on another ride. Brent, Sara, and I entered the tent without him and took seats down in the front.

The sign above the stage read, GREAT CHARACTERS OF LITERATURE. This made me feel better about being there. I jabbed Sara in the ribs and whispered to her, "It looks like this is a safe place to be right now. Who do you think they'll have from the world of literature?" I had no more than finished my question when a man in a white lab coat pushed clumsily through the curtains.

"You are about to witness some of the great experiments in our history. Behind this curtain is one of the marvels of the world," he said.

"First you will meet my associate, Dr. Jekyll. He has created a new soft drink that is better than anything on the market today. It is the kind of drink that can change your life. It is so good that you won't be able to control yourself. You will want more and more. And now, here is Dr. Jekyll," the scientist told us.

The curtain opened to reveal Dr. Jekyll standing behind a lab table. Tubes ran everywhere, and different colored liquids pulsed through them. A bottle of bubbly, bluish liquid stood in the middle of the table.

"All of us want to change something about ourselves. We either want to be taller or stronger, prettier or more outgoing. I have created a drink that takes

46

those internal desires and makes you into what you want to be," the doctor lectured.

I leaned over to Brent. "Not bad. I wish I would have had that last week at the football game. My internal desire was to be a tank and break through the other team's line. Do you think that I could be a tank after I drank that stuff?"

Brent laughed at my comment, and Dr. Jekyll glared at us. "Hey, you two just made him mad," Sara said. "I don't want to be a part of what causes him to come out here and gently remove our hearts. So just cool it!"

I sat up straight in my seat and so did Brent. The doctor continued his comments about his drink. I was getting a little bored and stopped watching just as the old guy raised the bottle to his lips. Then I heard Sara gasp.

I glanced at Sara, then looked back at the stage. Dr. Jekyll's body shook, and he jumped around the stage, screaming at the top of his voice. He raced from side to side, then off the side of the stage, then back on again. His appearance began to change.

Dropping to the floor, the doctor kicked his feet like he was having a temper tantrum. I leaned over to Brent and said, "Where are we? Baby-sitting your little brother?"

Brent broke out again in laughter. Bad move. Dr. Jekyll stood up. He had gone through a total transformation. A beastly set of eyes glared out from a twisted

47

and distorted face. His crooked body stepped around the lab table and started our way. He dragged his limp left leg behind him.

I started to panic. He was almost to the edge of the stage when the curtains closed and stopped his coming any closer to us.

"That was close," Brent sighed. Sara sighed, too.

The man in the lab coat walked out from the stage wings and smiled at us. "I'm so sorry. My friend Dr. Jekyll can't always control his emotions when he is being heckled." He smirked at us and continued. "I am so sorry I forgot to introduce myself. I am Dr. Frankenstein, and behind this curtain stands my creation."

The three of us looked at one another. This place had taken a wrong turn again. The curtains began to move a little, then a nonhuman voice cried out, "Argh!" The red velvet curtains drew open, and before us stood Frankenstein's monster.

# 12

Sara immediately stood up. "Quick, get out, get out!"

I was at the end of the row and out into the aisle as quickly as possible. The monster was only a few rows away from us.

He looked at us, then at Dr. Frankenstein.

The doctor tried to hold him back, but the monster swung his large arm at the doctor, knocking him to the stage. The monster headed toward us.

I turned to Brent and grabbed him by the arm. He was frozen with fear in his seat. Sara tried to get him to stand.

"Come on, Brent, let's get out of here," I yelled as I pulled him to his feet and out into the aisle. Sara pushed him and I pulled at him all the way to the exit doors.

As I reached the doors, all I could think about were the times that the doors to an amusement slid shut on us. I prayed that this time the doors would be open.

I spun my head around and saw that the monster

was only a few feet behind us. *The doors have to open,* I thought, *or we're all dead meat.*

My hand reached for the crash bar on the door. "Please, Lord, make them open," I prayed aloud. I pressed with all my weight against the metal door. Brent and Sara crashed against me.

I heard the monster's big feet thud on the ground right behind us. "Let's get out of—"

"He's got me," Sara screamed.

I turned my head quickly. For a moment I forgot the door. Something happened in my head. The only thing I could think to do was to karate chop the monster's arm. I leaped in the air, gave my best kung fu scream, and came down hard on the arm.

"Ow!" I yelled. The monster felt like it was made of steel. I looked the monster in the eyes. He was shocked and let go of Sara's arm.

By then, Brent had pushed open the door and we went flying into the sun, stumbling and falling into the dirt of the midway.

Sammy stood over us. "You guys didn't stay very long. Was the show that bad?"

I was breathing hard as I tried to explain. "A monster—Frankenstein—grabbed Sara—the door—" Sammy's face beamed. "Wow! I can't believe I missed all that fun. I'm not sitting out one more thing around this place. Everything is better than what it seems. Let's go back inside."

50

"Everything is weirder than it seems, you mean," Sara added. "I'm not going back inside for anything."

Brent caught his breath and stepped into the middle of us. "Listen, I'm not sure I know what's going on, but I want to do like Sara said and find out what's behind all this.

"Look! There's a Tilt-a-Whirl over there. That is my most favorite ride in the world. I'm going to go on it. I bet I've ridden that ride a hundred times. Nothing weird can happen on it."

Brent marched toward the ride before I could stop him. Dr. Shivers had been able to make everything else twice as frightening as it should be. I was sure that the Tilt-a-Whirl wouldn't be any different.

"Wait up, Brent. If you're going on that ride we all are. From now on, we better hang together," I called after him.

"Or we'll hang alone," Sara said gloomily, reminding us all of the clown's noose.

The Tilt-a-Whirl was a basic spinning ride that rose and fell on small hills. Sometimes it went very fast. I always liked it, too.

But everything at Dr. Shivers' Carnival of Terror was unpredictable. I recalled what had happened on the merry-go-round. I had little hope that the Tilt-a-Whirl would be any different.

Brent was the first one on. Sammy and Sara climbed on after. I looked around for spiders, Frankenstein's monster, barking hot dogs, or strange clowns. I didn't

51

see anything or anybody, not even a person to run the ride. I cautiously got on.

When I sat down, the safety bar dropped and secured us in. The ride began to move slowly, then faster and faster.

"You would think that Dr. Shivers would come up with something different. We've already gone fast. We've already been trapped on rides," Sammy said with disappointment in his voice.

Then he startled us all by yelling, "Dr. Shivers, this ride isn't very frightening!"

"It will be!" came a voice from the loudspeaker over the Tilt-a-Whirl cars.

"Thanks, Sammy. Thanks a lot," I said. "Now he's going to make this one more frightening than all the others."

The entire ride began to sink into the ground. It was lowered a foot every couple of seconds until we were in some kind of pit. Ghostly faces appeared along the walls of the pit.

"We've got to get out of the seat!" I screamed.

"Not now, or the centrifugal force of us spinning so fast will toss you several hundred feet. Stay in the car. I'll figure something out," Sara screamed back to me.

We went down another three feet. The carnival had disappeared from sight. Gremlins and skeletons raced next to our car. This ride was too weird, way too weird.

Then it suddenly slowed down and started to rise toward the surface again. Once we were back at the top, the car stopped and the safety bar opened. I looked up, and at the controls of the ride was the clown.

He was wearing the noose around his neck.

"It's him!" Brent yelled. "It's the clown. Run for your lives."

The Tilt-a-Whirl had barely stopped when we hit the ground and headed as far away from it and the clown as possible.

Unfortunately, it was also away from the gate leading out of the carnival. I kept looking back, but the clown wasn't following us.

Sammy turned down an alley of the midway. "I think the gate out is this way," he yelled back to us.

We all followed him, running as fast as we could. Then he jammed his high-tops into the dirt so quickly that I thought we all were going to run into him.

I saw why he stopped so suddenly.

There before us was a stage. On the stage was a ventriloquist with his dummy. The dummy was dressed in a plaid shirt and bib overalls. The ventriloquist wore a dark suit and a red bow tie. The marked difference in their attire made them look a little funny.

We stared at them.

"Hello, kids," the dummy said. "It's time for another terrible show, knot. Get it? Knot." He chuckled and pointed to the ventriloquist's bow tie as he spoke.

"Hey, kids. I went to the doctor the other day because I thought I caught the flu bug. He said, here's something for the bug and he gave me a woodpecker. Get it? Woodpecker. Ha, ha, ha. I've got a million of them."

Sammy laughed right along with him. I shifted from foot to foot. This whole place made me feel tense. Nothing here was what it was supposed to be.

Nothing turned out the way it should.

Nothing made sense.

I knew I wasn't looking at it from the right perspective, but I wasn't sure what the right perspective was. If it was a dream or something in a book, then all this stuff would be understandable, even funny.

But this wasn't a book. It wasn't TV. It wasn't a dream. I, Kyle Conlon, was living through a real, live, crazy adventure.

Sara snapped me from my thoughts when she asked the dummy a question. "Would you tell us some more jokes?"

"Wood I? Get it? Wood eye. Ha, ha, ha. I got a million of them," the dummy answered, pointing to his eyeball.

The ventriloquist looked at us and smiled. His teeth

55

were white and perfectly straight. His blue eyes had a blank look, as if there was little behind them.

"I've got a better idea. Instead of more jokes, how about a nice trick or two? I will need a volunteer from the audience."

Sara leaped to the stage. "I'm ready. What do I need to do?"

"Come closer, my friend," said the dummy. "I need you to put your hands at your side and close your eyes. Now, I'm going to place something around your neck—like my hands."

I had a bad feeling about this, and it was confirmed when the dummy leaped off the ventriloquist's lap and onto Sara. The force of the dummy hitting her knocked Sara to the stage.

It didn't look like the ventriloquist threw him. From my viewpoint, I thought the dummy jumped on his own.

But dummies don't do anything on their own. The ventriloquist does all the moving.

This dummy was operating on his own as if he were alive.

The dummy's wooden hands and fingers closed tightly around Sara's neck. "Help me, somebody," Sara cried with fear as she gasped for breath.

I cupped my hands around my mouth and yelled loudly to the ventriloquist. He was doing nothing about his dummy's attack.

I leaped onto the stage and raced up to him. I pushed

56

him on the arm to get his attention, but the ventriloquist slumped into the chair.

Then he slid off, making a heavy wooden thud on the stage. He was lifeless, and I saw the joints in his jawbone. They were hinged together by bolts.

He was the dummy.

## 14

Whatever was choking my friend Sara was not a dummy. It was alive, and Sara needed help.

Sammy witnessed what happened with the ventriloquist and jumped onto the stage. He was thinking like I was. We both dove for the mysterious fiend at the same time but smacked our heads hard against each other.

I tumbled off the back of the stage. Sammy rolled off the front. We groaned while Sara gasped, "Help!"

Brent moved so quickly that by the time I was able to pull my aching head and body onto the stage again, he was reaching for the imposter dummy. The moment his hands grabbed the menace, it went limp. We stared at the body, now lying lifeless on the stage. It, too, was made of wood.

"Thanks, Brent. I was beginning to think that you three were drawing straws to see who had to help me," Sara said as she sucked in some deep breaths. "I thought I was a goner for sure."

"I don't get it," Brent said. "This was a dummy, too. How could it have acted so lifelike?"

"I don't know," I said. "But I don't think I want to hang around here and find out."

Sammy seemed mesmerized by the experience, as though he had just witnessed nothing more than a magic trick. "So what's next?" he asked.

"Nothing!" Brent and I said simultaneously. We had had enough of this mania and wanted to leave.

Sammy stomped his feet in a mock temper tantrum. "I don't want to go, I don't want to go."

Sara added, "I don't think we should stay any longer. Let's just get out of here. I think the gate is this way." She started walking and we all fell in with her.

"Okay," Sammy said, "but if we leave now we'll never solve the mystery of Dr. Shivers' Carnival of Terror."

Brent stepped in to add his two cents worth. "I don't care. I'm out of here."

"There is something really strange going on around here," Sara said. "I wish we could figure it out. But frankly, I'm too spooked to stay."

"Do you think it's magic?" I asked.

"I'm not sure. After a few hours here I'm not sure of anything anymore," Sara answered with a puzzled look on her face.

Sammy wanted to make sure that we knew where he stood. "I love this place. I'm thinking of coming back tomorrow when it opens up. I feel like I've missed some of the best stuff. Besides, I've got to get one of those barking hot dogs to take back home with us. I've got to scare my little brother with it."

"What a guy. I don't ever want to see this place again. Tomorrow is too soon. Next week is too soon. Next month is too soon. Next—"

I stopped Brent in the middle of his sentence. I heard something.

We were only thirty feet from the gate when I heard footsteps, lots of footsteps heading our way. We spun around and saw a large crowd of people stampeding toward us. They must have been carnival workers, because several clowns were in the crowd.

They must have known we were getting ready to leave. Dr. Shivers' gang was going to make sure that we didn't depart.

As they got closer, the four of us jumped out of the way. They didn't even slow down. They ran right by us.

Why would they race as fast as they could our way and then not grab us? It didn't make sense.

Then I saw the reason. A large, roaring lion bounded around the corner. His hungry eyes looked directly at us.

I looked around. Our only escape was to enter the closest amusement to us. The door to it was only three feet away. The lion was about twenty feet away.

I had no choice. I grabbed Brent and Sammy by the arms and yelled to Sara. In two seconds we were falling backward through the door of a place called the Mummy's Tomb.

As hard as we were trying to leave, we weren't very successful.

The inside looked like the set of an Egyptian movie. Fake sandstone blocks were stacked along the walls. Flat human forms with their arms bent funny were painted on the blocks. It didn't look very scary.

Sara looked around at the paintings. "Hey, this could be really educational. I've been doing research on ancient Egypt for a report, so I can say that I did research on my Christmas vacation."

"Yeah, research on how to get scared to death," Brent tossed in.

"What I'm scared of right now is that lion outside. At least we're safe from it in here. Besides, maybe I can learn something," Sara said.

"About all you're going to learn is how to make a cheesy movie set. Let's just leave," I said.

"If you want to be eaten by a lion, go ahead. I'm staying in here a while," she answered.

Sara had a point. Our options were to stay inside the Mummy's Tomb or leave and risk becoming lunch for a hungry lion.

"You're right," I said. "We're safer in here than out there. I don't see anything in here that looks threatening."

With that matter solved, we descended a staircase. Behind large panes of glass we saw wax mummies authentically positioned in their tombs. Interesting historical facts were printed on metal plaques next to each window.

Sammy was bored. "Hey, let's hurry it along here."

We descended more stairs and passed more and more windows. After about forty steps I stopped everyone. "Have any of you noticed the same thing I noticed?"

Brent was the first to answer. "Yeah, why are we going downstairs? How could we go any deeper? This carnival was put up just last night while we slept. Nobody would have had time to dig out a hole this deep. Now I've got the shivers."

"This whole place gives me the shivers," I added.

Sammy chimed in, "Yeah, Dr. Shivers."

"Let's turn around and get out of here," Brent said. "I don't think that there is anything else worth seeing. That lion's got to be gone by now."

"I'm with Brent," I said. With that, I turned to walk back up the stairs.

I froze.

My voice caught in my throat and my mouth went dry.

Only three steps away from me was a figure wrapped in cloth strips. It was a mummy.

**16**

My friends twisted their heads quickly and saw the mummy standing behind me.

My mouth was wide open. After everything we had seen I should have been ready for another fright. I wasn't. No one else was either.

We had been looking at all the glass-encased wax mummies and didn't expect that a real one would suddenly appear behind us.

I was still trying to form words when Brent screamed, "Run, everybody, run!"

Holding on to the rail for balance, we took three steps at a time down the staircase. How many more steps we took I don't know. I was too frightened to count, and the mummy was bounding down behind us. The wrappings kept it from moving too fast, and that may have saved us.

The monster yelled, "You have violated my tomb. You are cursed. You must die."

His eerie, deep rough voice was enough to keep us running.

Sammy stumbled when he hit bottom. He fell against the wall and slipped to the floor.

Sara leaped over him to keep from tripping, but Brent wasn't so lucky. He went sprawling along the ground as well. I was able to stop myself in front of them.

"Quick, get up. We don't have time for a rest," I yelled.

"Who's resting?" Brent answered. "This guy fell, and I tripped over him. Help us up."

"You have violated my tomb." The voice was closer as it called to us.

"This way!" Sara yelled. "I've found another room."

Sammy scrambled to his feet as I pulled Brent to his. "We've got to find a way out of here. I don't think this guy likes houseguests," I said to the others.

Even Sammy was nervous now. He shot back, "Another brilliant deduction, Sherlock. I really don't need you to give me a running commentary of what is going on. I just want to get out of here."

We raced behind Sara into the big room. All around us were gold chalices, jewelry, and gold-covered statues with human bodies and animal heads. It was really strange.

"Great," Sammy snapped at Sara. "Now, we're trapped in some room with no way out. We've got an angry mummy that doesn't plan on just grounding us but putting us into the ground and there isn't a way out. Can this get any worse?"

"You have violated my tomb. You must die." The mummy sounded very close.

"I think it just got worse. He's outside the door to this room," Sara said.

I yelled instructions to everyone. "Quick, grab some of those statues and push them in front of the door. It will keep him out for a few minutes. Brent, start looking for a way out of here."

Brent panicked. "Like what, Kyle?"

"A button, a switch. Anything that might move a wall. All of Dr. Shivers' amusements have had a trick to get out. Look for the one here."

Brent felt along the walls while the rest of us pushed statues across the door. After the third one, I felt we might keep the mummy out long enough to find an escape.

The mummy appeared at the door. "You cannot stop me. I must kill you. You have violated my tomb," he called to us in his low raspy voice.

I didn't want to stick around to find out whether he meant it or not. I began pushing on the walls. I thought that there might be a fake wall or a trapdoor or a hidden door.

Brent pulled everything in sight to see if some object would open up a sliding door to another passageway.

Sammy and Sara piled more Egyptian artifacts in front of the door to keep the mummy out.

The mummy continued to yell, "You have violated my tomb. You must die."

Sammy ran toward me. As he neared me, his foot caught in an Egyptian necklace and he tripped. His body soared through the air then hit a casket. As he fell back away from it, the door to the casket popped open. A dim light shone from somewhere deep within the casket.

Brent turned and yelled, "Sammy, what did you do?"

I didn't have time to see the damage caused by his fall. Our mummy friend pushed through the statues in front of the doorway and was stepping over them.

Soon he would have us in his grasp.

"We're doomed!" I yelled.

**17**

Sara jumped out of the mummy's way and headed right toward us, then made a quick cut and ran for the open casket. "Follow me and don't ask questions," she called as she raced by.

Sammy and Brent bumped into each other as they dove through the casket door. I turned to see where the mummy was. My delay cost me big time. His large, wrapped hands grabbed me by the shoulders. I was only inches from the casket.

Four hands reached from inside the casket and grabbed me. *No, no*, I thought. *I'm part of a mummy tug-of-war*. I could see the newspaper headline now: BOY TORN APART BY HIS MUMMIES. I was scared.

The four hands inside the casket won the battle, pulling me hard into another room. I was moving so fast that I fell over my captors and facedown onto the dirty floor. Rolling over, I opened my eyes.

It couldn't be.

I was lying between Sammy and Sara in the dusty

dirt of another room in the tomb. "Thanks. That one was really close. I was not sure if I was ever going to get out of the mummy's hands. Do you have any idea where we are?"

"I have not had time to look around, but this appears to be the room where they prepared the mummies for burial. If I'm right, there will be a secret door here that leads to the outside. The people who prepared the mummies needed a way out that couldn't be seen by grave robbers," Sara explained.

"Let's get going. I want out of here as quickly as possible," Brent added.

Each of us searched the room for the secret door. Sammy climbed the rocks that jutted out from the wall to search the ceiling, while Sara searched the floor. Brent felt along the stone wall.

"Nothing. There is nothing here," Sara said with frustration in her voice.

"Keep looking, Sara. We have to find a way out. Besides, that mummy knows all the ways into this place. I would not be surprised if he mysteriously showed up out of the shadows. So keep looking," Brent insisted.

She went back to feeling and tugging on each rock. Brent pushed every painted symbol on the wall. There wasn't much light inside our mummy's preparation room.

A torch on the wall gave us enough to see, but that most likely would not last as long as we needed it.

Sara stood up and straightened her spine. "I'm getting sore bending over. I wish we were back at your uncle's house relaxing in the hot tub, Kyle."

"I want to swim in the pool and get some of this dirt off me," Sammy called down from his search of the high points of the wall.

"That's it. Keep thinking about getting back to my uncle's," I said like a cheerleader rallying the team.

By that point, Brent was so afraid that he couldn't muster any optimism. "Kyle, you are assuming that we *will* get out of here. So far, I have seen nothing that leads me to believe we will ever see your uncle's house or Carverville or our parents ever again."

Sara walked over to him and touched his shoulder. "We're all a little scared by this. But you'll see, we will find the way out. Most likely one of us will do it by accident."

The torchlight was getting dimmer. I needed to do something to stretch our lighting. While the others looked for the passage, I went through the bottles of fluids and stone boxes.

If I could find a liquid that burned, I would dip the old cloth strips in it and wrap that around a torch. I saw this in a movie once.

It worked for the hero on the big screen. I hoped it would work for me as well.

There was one large vial on the top shelf over the stone table used for the mummification process. I grabbed it, but I couldn't lift it off the shelf. Instead, it fell forward as if it were hinged.

I stood on tiptoe to get a better look, when all of a sudden a horrible grinding noise made me spin around.

"What's that noise? What's happening?" I hurriedly said to the others.

"That large stone over there is moving," Brent answered fearfully.

We all watched as a square piece of stone about the size of a refrigerator began to slide forward. As it inched toward us, I felt the hairs rise on the back of my neck and chills ran up and down my spine. What could this be? What would come out of there?

**18**

A hand curled around the stone. It was wrapped heavily in cloth strips. I was sure that our mummy was coming again.

Sara jumped back and bumped into Brent, who was already retreating. When her body struck Brent's, he stumbled over some stones on the floor of the room and lost his balance. Brent hit the ground hard. I heard the thud and raced toward him.

Sammy leaped away from the wall and grabbed a wooden beam. From there he swung like a monkey to a torch holder. When he grabbed the torch holder it gave way and flipped downward.

By accident, Sammy had found the hidden lever that opened the secret passage to the outside.

Unfortunately, the mummy was already slipping in the other passageway and three of us were lying on the floor.

I yanked hard on Brent's arm and pulled him to his feet. Sara was already scrambling up, and Sammy's tumble to the ground lasted only a second.

We had to get out of there before the mummy made it to us. I didn't know what this mummy wanted to do to us, but I was certain he didn't intend to give us a loving hug.

Brent was still groggy from his fall. I guided him toward the passageway and pushed his body through. He stumbled again and fell. Inside the opening was another staircase.

Sara and I hoisted Brent up. Sara supported Brent's weight under one arm and I took the other. We began to drag him up the steps.

Sammy was left with the unfortunate job of holding the mummy back until we climbed the stairs. I don't know what he did but whatever it was, it worked.

The three of us had reached the top when I heard Sammy's shoes slapping the stone stairway. He was only a few inches behind us as we turned the corner and discovered ourselves at a fork in the staircase.

The mummy was halfway up the steps. We heard him shouting his favorite and only phrase, "You have violated my tomb. You must die."

"Which way do we go?" I asked the others.

Sara thought a moment and said, "Left."

Sammy said, "Right."

"We only have a few more seconds to make the decision here. Which way?" I pressed for one unified answer.

Brent stood on his own now and studied the stairways. "Definitely left," he said.

"That's good enough for me." I reached to help Brent up the steps, but it was obvious he no longer needed help. The four of us ran up the stairs.

I was near the top of the staircase when I looked behind me to see where my friends were. I should have been looking ahead, because as I hit the top landing my body crunched into another one.

I looked up. It was the mummy. His big hands locked me in a tight hold. He said over and over again, "You have violated my tomb. You must die." He really meant it.

"Don't come the rest of the way up the stairs!" I yelled, panic straining my voice. My friends stopped below me.

"What do we do?" Sammy asked.

Sara didn't wait to find out what the others were going to say. She ran as fast as she could back down the steps.

The mummy dragged me along the hallway. I twisted from side to side, trying to break free, but the mummy was too strong. He picked me up and slung me over his shoulder.

I could hear Brent panicking. "It's my fault! I chose this staircase. Kyle's going to die, and it's my fault!"

The mummy turned a bend in the corridor, then halted. I did not know if that was a good or bad sign. I twisted around to see what had caused him to stop.

Sara stood in front of us with a flaming torch. "All right, mummy. There is nothing that this blazing, fiery torch would like more than to set fire to a bunch of old rags wrapped around some two-thousand-year-old, withered body. So, drop my friend and you go free."

The move was extremely bold. And it worked. The mummy hurried away to some other part of his Egyptian tomb. Sara had saved my life. "Hurry!" she said, not waiting for me to thank her. "Let's get back to the staircase."

Sara and I ran back down the hall and found Brent and Sammy seemingly frozen on the steps, their eyes opened wide in fear. When Brent saw me he let out a wail, "Kyle. Oh, Kyle, I thought you were—"

"Come on," I interrupted. "No time for that now. Let's get moving."

We raced to the bottom of the steps and got to the other staircase. We climbed it to the top. We walked another few steps and came to a dead end in the stone-lined hallway. There was no way out.

"I can't figure this out," I said. "One of these stairways should have led us to the secret passage out of here." I turned to tell the others that we needed to go back.

There was no one behind me. My friends had vanished.

# 19

"Sara! Sammy! Brent!" I called their names, but no answer came back to me. They were right behind me only a moment before.

I imagined that the mummy had grabbed them. I needed to save them, but how could just one kid beat a two-thousand-year-old monster? Feeling helpless and hopeless, I slumped down in the corner.

For the first time that day I felt like crying. I wanted out of this mummy's tomb and out of the carnival.

I stood up and started back down the dark passageway. I moved slowly and quietly until I heard voices. I stopped.

My heart beat so loudly that I could not hear what was being said. I knew I needed to go closer, but I was too scared. For several moments I stood silently, leaning against the stone wall.

Then I pulled together all the courage I had and made a step toward the voices. The voices were barely audible, but I recognized them as the voices of Sammy, Sara, and Brent.

Sammy whispered, "The mummy must have grabbed Kyle. He was up ahead of us and then he was gone. I think we need to go back and look for him."

"How are we going to look for him? We don't have a torch since Sara's burned out. We don't have a flashlight. We don't have any idea where he might be," Brent said.

"That does not make any difference to me. Kyle is lost and we need to find him," Sara objected to Brent's statements. "Besides we have come to a dead end. This passage leads nowhere."

They were in the same predicament that I was in. I went down another corridor that led to nowhere and so did they. If the ones we chose did not lead to safety then there must not be a way out. Or there must be another passage we did not see or feel as we traveled along the stone hallway.

"Let's go find him," Sara said. I could hear her footsteps coming toward me. The others were right behind her. Their steps sounded so close to me. I was going to reach out and grab Sammy. That ought to pay him back for all the practical jokes that he pulled on me.

I waited, but their steps never got any closer. In fact, they now headed away from me. The three must have found the passageway out. I had to catch up to them.

I started down the corridor, feeling my way along the rocks. I moved slowly, touching from side to side.

I knew that if I could feel the opening I would find my friends. It was my only hope.

After a few minutes, I thought that I should have found the passage opening. I started to get frightened. I should have called to them before.

I felt from one side to the other.

My right hand touched stone. My left hand touched stone.

My right hand touched stone. My left hand touched rags.

I pulled it away quickly. What was that? I heard deep, heavy breathing, then a growling whisper that moved closer and closer to my ear.

"You have violated my tomb. You must die."

# 20

"Aah!" I shrieked. I backed away from the monster. When I did that I felt no stone behind me. The passageway was right there.

The monster's hand reached out and grabbed me, but it didn't get a good hold on me. I broke free and went hurtling down the open corridor behind me.

The mummy's cloth-wrapped feet thudded along the stones. It was too close for me to feel safe.

"Help! Sammy, Sara, Brent, where are you? The mummy is right behind me. We need to get out of here and we need to do it right now."

"Kyle, run toward my voice," Sara yelled.

She was close, but I suddenly realized how stupid I was. I had just led the mummy right to my friends. We had not found the way out yet. The mummy was inches away from me.

In the dark, I could not tell how close I was to them. I found out soon enough, when I slammed into them and we all went flying into the rocks at the end of the stone hallway.

When we hit the wall I felt it move slightly and then pop open. The sunlight bathed us as we tumbled to the dirt midway of Dr. Shivers' Carnival of Terror. We had to shut our eyes to protect them from the brightness.

Brent let out a long breath. Sara gasped for breath. I was confused. Sammy had a very different response from the rest of us and a very typical one for him. He was giggling.

"That was great," Sammy said. "I like this place more and more every time we go into another amusement."

"Maybe you like it so much because you weren't grabbed by a mummy," I snapped back at him as I stood dusting myself off.

"Or because you didn't eat any worms crawling inside of cotton candy," Brent added.

"And you didn't get strangled by a living dummy," Sara threw in for good measure. "I vote that we get out of here," Sara said as she moved into the center of our group and looked each of us in the eyes. I was with her all the way.

Then Sammy piped up again. "But I still want a prize before we go. There's a ball toss over there. Let me do that and then we can get out of here quickly." Sammy ran toward the game booth before any of us had time to respond.

A barker appeared as we approached the game. He

had a big beaming smile. "What can I do for you? Do you want to win a prize?" he asked.

"That's what we're here for. What do we have to do, sir?" Sammy asked.

"Simple, my friends. Just knock over the bottles in three tries," the barker answered.

Sammy picked up the balls, but then paused. He looked at Sara. "You're the best pitcher here. Why don't you try? If you win will you let me keep the prize?"

"All right," Sara agreed. "Anything to get out of here quickly."

Sara tossed the first ball. It hit the bottles and the top one fell off. The next time she hit the center one and they all fell but one. On her third attempt the last bottle fell.

"You won," Brent shouted, "but where did the guy go?"

"Right here, I just had to get the prize." His back was to us. When he turned around, his beaming smile had turned into bloodstained fangs. His face was covered with dripping green skin, and his eyes glowed bright red.

**21**

"Aah!" we yelled in unison.

The barker laughed and gripped his face with his hands. He pulled off a mask. He was now howling with laughter. "That gets them every time. I love doing that to kids," he said through his laughing teeth.

Sammy grabbed the mask right away, but Brent took it from his hands.

Brent put it on and tried to scare us all with it. After what we had been through a little mask didn't seem to have much effect.

He threw it to Sara to try on next. She declined and so did I. Sammy waited patiently, or at least as patiently as he could.

When Brent handed the mask to Sammy he slipped it over his head. He goofed off a little with it then went to remove it.

"Hey, I can't get it off," Sammy cried out.

"Quit goofing off, Samuel," Brent said very seriously.

"I agree," I said with emphasis.

"Help me. It feels like it is sticking to my skin. It's starting to feel like my skin. Quick, help me," Sammy whimpered.

His body started to twist away from us. I thought he was in pain. Suddenly he stood straight up with his back to us.

I felt relieved that he seemed to be back to himself. Sammy turned very slowly. His arms were raised in the air. His eyes were red and horrible looking. He spoke to us, "Dr. Shivers has sent me to eliminate all of you. I must do as the good doctor says."

The mask had been loose when Sammy first put it on. Now it was drawn tightly over his face and neck.

He took a step toward us. We huddled together. I don't know what the others were thinking, but I was torn. *Do I help my friend or do I run for my life?*

I turned to the other two. "Sara, you and I will hold Sammy down while Brent pulls off the mask." They nodded in agreement

We lunged at Sammy. Sara and I held Sammy on the ground while Brent pounced on Sammy's chest. Brent grabbed for the mask and I heard Sammy laugh.

"Got you, didn't I?" he said.

It was the first time I ever saw Brent want to hit anybody. He formed a fist with his right hand and grimaced, but he held back.

"I guess I shouldn't have done that. I'm sorry,

everyone. This place even has me caught up in its frightening antics. I'm ready to leave if all of you are."

We climbed off Sammy. Sara and I helped him up. But Brent had been distracted. He stood staring at the amusement next to the ball toss. The sign read, THE COFFIN CHALLENGE.

The man standing by the gate of the Coffin Challenge motioned for us to come over.

"No thank you, sir," I responded, because I thought we were leaving.

The man smiled and shrugged off my statement. He started to explain the challenge. "It's easy, kids. All you do is challenge your friends. The one who can lie in the coffin the longest wins a prize. Now there is one catch. We close the coffin. But all you have to do is push the button on this remote control, and *presto!* it opens. Not too hard is it? The one who stays in the longest wins."

"What do we win?" Sammy asked.

"Any prize on our shelf," he fired back.

The shelf was filled with great stuffed animals—and a stuffed Dr. Shivers. I wanted to win that just so I could use it as a punching bag.

There was even a portable CD player. I could sure use that as well. I wanted it more than I wanted to punch the good doctor.

I surprised even myself as I walked toward the coffins. My desire for that CD player was greater than my desire to leave.

84

"Jump right in now. I'll close these lids and the four of you can take the challenge," the man said eagerly.

We climbed in. My coffin was soft and comfortable. *I could use a rest*, I thought. If I had fallen asleep I probably could have made the *Guinness Book of World Records* for the longest time a living person spent in a coffin. Although, I don't think Guinness has a category like that.

The lids closed on the four of us. Soft organ music began to play outside the coffin. It sounded like music from a funeral parlor. *Very fitting*, I thought.

I was starting to doze off when I felt the coffin move downward. The coffin moved lower, then lower again. It came to a stop. Something began to pelt the coffin lid. I suddenly realized someone was shoveling dirt on the coffin. *I only wanted a rest, not to rest in peace*, I thought.

I pressed the button.

Nothing happened.

I pressed it again. Still nothing happened.

The lid didn't open, and the dirt started falling heavier and heavier onto the lid. I was scared. It was pitch black inside the coffin.

I pressed the button again. I waited for the lid to open. It didn't. Then I heard Brent screaming in the coffin next to me. Sara was on the other side, and I heard her yelling and kicking. We were all frightened.

We were being buried alive!

## 22

I frantically kicked at the coffin lid, but the activity started to use up the air inside my padded graveyard condo. It was getting more uncomfortable inside the coffin by the minute.

I heard the others pounding and kicking. Sammy's screams for help were louder than all the others. I couldn't believe that even he was scared. He had acted like this place was one fun amusement after another.

It really was a carnival of terror. Dr. Shivers had named it correctly.

I kicked again and again. The dirt had stopped falling, but the lid hadn't opened. Maybe the man outside couldn't hear us because the dirt was too thick.

Or maybe he planned to bury us.

We would probably end up as mummies in the Mummy's Tomb. These thoughts scared me and I had to stop them. I kicked again.

My lid popped open. I jumped up and saw all three

of my friends jumping out of their coffins at the same time. The man ran up to us.

"I'm so sorry. I suddenly remembered that I didn't put batteries in the remote controls this morning. My deepest apologies. Please don't say anything to Dr. Shivers. He'll have my head if you do," he pleaded with us.

"That's okay," Brent said. "We know the kind of guy Dr. Shivers is, and we know that he will certainly have your head—"

"Most likely for breakfast," Sammy butted in.

He continued his apology. "If you don't say anything then I'll get you into Dracula's Castle."

"We can get on anything we want for free," I told him.

"Not the castle. It isn't quite finished yet, but it is truly a great amusement. You'll be the first ever. It is a barrel of laughs. I promise it will drive you batty," he said in a fast, frantic voice.

"It's a deal," Sammy said.

The three of us shot Sammy a nasty look. We wanted to go home. Now we had to try Dracula's Castle.

Brent looked at the castle and turned to us. "Hey, they've got something like this at Go-Go Lake. The place was filled with lots of wax monsters. It wasn't so scary."

The operator unlocked the door and ushered us in.

"You'll love it. It really is neat. I promise it will drive you batty," he said as he closed us in.

When he closed the door, the room went black.

"So where are the wax people, Brent?" I asked disgustedly.

"Just wait a minute, Kyle, the lights will come on and you'll see them," he said.

We waited a minute and nothing happened. "Let's find the door and get out of here," Sara said. I agreed with her, and we started moving in the blackness toward what we hoped were walls.

I bumped into something and it moved. I screamed. It screamed back. I recognized the scream. Sammy and I laughed at each other. I was ready to say something funny when I heard a strange noise.

Brent spoke first. "What's that noise?"

"Bats," said Sara.

"*What?* I hate bats. Please, tell me those aren't bats," Brent pleaded.

"I thought you hated spiders," Sammy said.

"Spiders and bats. I hate both of them," Brent responded.

"That guy said this place would drive us batty, and I think he meant it," Sammy said.

A dim light came on in the middle of the room. It shone on a tall man wearing a black cape. When he grinned, two long fangs edged over his bottom lip. I had seen enough scary movies to know who this was. "It's Dracula!" I yelled.

Suddenly the glowing light went out then appeared in another part of the room, again illuminating the figure of Dracula. Then Dracula's light went out again and appeared on the other side of the room.

This guy was fast. He made the Olympic runners look slow.

The next time Dracula appeared, I used the light to find the wall. I kept low because the sound of flying bats was all around us. I could barely see Brent swatting in the air at them.

"Hey, the next time he appears head toward me," I cried out. They heard me. On his next appearance they all ran toward me.

Unfortunately, Count Dracula heard me as well. His next appearance was right next to us.

He reached out for Brent. He was inches from his neck. Dracula's mouth opened to reveal those long fangs.

He wanted dinner, and Brent, a healthy red-blooded American boy, must have looked delicious.

# 23

Brent jumped back against us and we all slammed against the wall. The wall fell away. Sunlight flooded the room.

There was no Count Dracula and there were no bats.

"This place gets better as we go along," Sammy said.

Sara looked at him like he was crazy. "I would like to leave. Which way is out?"

"I kind of remember that the front gate was over there by that balloon stand. We all can get one of those really scary balloons and head back to Kyle's uncle's. I think I've got enough stories to tell about this place, but the balloon will make it fun to show all the kids back in Carverville. Besides, we can ask that balloon vendor where the gate is," Brent told us.

"To the balloons!" Sara yelled, and I raced toward the booth. I stopped dead in my tracks in front of it. The balloons were there, but the vendor wasn't.

A moment before, a woman dressed in a bright red jacket had been standing next to the balloons smiling at us. Now she was gone.

Sara ran up behind me. She laughed and said, "I'm second." Then she gasped. "Where is the woman who was here a minute ago?"

"That's what I was just thinking. I saw her, and I don't remember taking my eyes off the balloons. How could she have slipped away so quickly? Let's just skip the balloons and get out of this place," I told her.

Brent was with us next. "Let's at least get a balloon," he said.

"All right. But after this I'm going home," I told him firmly.

"We've all said that and then something else happens to keep us in here. I'm beginning to think that this is not an easy place to get out of. At least to leave alive," Sara added.

The three of us starting pulling at the balloon strings. Sara chose one that had Dracula painted on it. She said it was because of our chance meeting in his castle. Hers came out easily.

Brent's was a little tougher. He tugged and tugged on the string of a face that looked more like a monster than most monster masks in stores. It came loose, and he stood waiting for me.

My choice was a little less frightening. It was a cute little animal face. My problem was that my string wouldn't come loose at all. The three of us grabbed the string and yanked it. It wouldn't budge.

"I surrender. I'll take something else." The moment I said that, the balloon popped loose and started floating in the air. We all jumped for it, but the helium was lighter than we were and the balloon continued to rise.

"This is just not my day. I can't even get a balloon without something strange happening. I'll try again." I walked back to the group of balloons, but my eyes were still focused on the one I lost.

Bang!

"Somebody is shooting at us again," Brent said. "Hit the dirt!"

We were on the ground in a second.

"Who is shooting at us?" Sara asked. She was quiet for a minute and then cried out, "Where's Sammy? Where did he go? Have either one of you two seen him?"

I sat up and stared around, but I didn't see Sammy. I yelled for him, "Sammy, where are you? Quit goofing around, Sammy. Come on, don't joke around like this." No answer. I climbed to my feet just as another shot rang out.

Bang!

Before I could hit the ground again, the balloon I originally wanted dropped broken on my head. I grabbed it off my head and looked up.

I saw a piece of paper floating to the ground. It must

have been inside the balloon. The shot must have been to break the balloon.

"What is it?" Brent asked.

I picked up the paper. "It's a message to us. I think it has something to do with Sammy."

Sara grabbed the paper out of my hand.

"What does it say, Sara?" Brent asked.

"'We have something that you may want back. Come to the Tunnel of the Weird.'"

"What do you think it means?" I asked.

"I think you were right. I think someone has kidnapped Sammy and we have to get him back. He is probably at this Tunnel of the Weird," Sara said.

"Where is the tunnel?" I asked.

"I haven't seen anything like that or any name like that anywhere in the carnival," Brent said.

"We better split up and look for it. I don't think we have much time. We need to find him now," Sara said firmly.

"I think we should ask someone where it is," Brent said.

"Where are we going to find someone to ask?" I snapped.

Brent looked around, his eyes growing wider and wider. "Over there," he said.

Sara and I turned around quickly on our heels.

It was the clown.

# 24

The clown lifted his arm and waved. He motioned to us to follow him. Then he started to move down another midway of rides and games, ones that we had not seen before.

He stayed about ten feet ahead of us. I didn't mind that. He was a strange character to say the least.

The clown passed a lemonade stand and turned right, disappearing from our sight. By the time we got around the corner, he was gone. I wasn't sure where to look for him.

There were several rides and other amusements that he could have slipped into. It didn't make any difference where he had gone. We were looking for the Tunnel of the Weird.

"I see it over there," Sara said, pointing straight ahead. The sign over the entrance looked old, and it hung by one rusty nail from one side. The wind was making it swing back and forth. We heard it squeak.

"Do you hear that?" I asked.

"What?" Sara said.

"We can hear the sign squeaking."

Sara looked at me like I was crazy.

"The music from the public address system has been turned off. I'm beginning to think that this Tunnel of the Weird is not a safe place for any of us," I said fearfully.

Brent put his hand on my shoulder, then stepped toward the tunnel. "We do not have a choice in this situation. Sammy has been snatched away from us and we need to find him."

"I'm all for it, but I think we should have some sort of game plan," Sara added.

"I've got one. Let's go in and get Sammy and get back out alive," Brent said matter-of-factly. "We don't know what is in there. We need to stay close to one another and grab Sammy as soon as we can.

"It will be my job to guide us in. Sara, you will guide us out. Kyle will take the lead against any monster that we might find in there. Agreed?"

"I'm ready," Sara said.

"Me, too," I chirped.

We walked the few feet toward the tunnel with slow, fearful steps. The entrance was a heavy, dark brown wooden door. We slowly pushed our way through it.

Inside, it was very dark. I could hear an amusement ride car on a track near me.

"Let me get in the lead. This is my part of the plan,"

Brent said as he moved by me. "Can anyone see the cars for the ride?"

"Over here, children." The voice came out of the dark. My eyes had adjusted to the dark by now. A soft glowing light lit the face of a man on the other side of the tracks.

He continued, "Welcome to the Tunnel of the Weird. Many go in. Few come out. Would you have a seat please?"

The bar to the car popped up and the three of us climbed in. I looked at the man and asked, "What do you mean by 'few come out'?" He didn't answer. In another moment the car lurched forward. I turned back to look at the man, but he was gone. We were entering the tunnel.

Brent relaxed. "I've seen this ride before. They have it at the Big America Theme Park."

"What happens?" Sara quizzed.

"I don't know for sure. I mean, I've never ridden the one at Big America. I've only seen it. I've heard that a bunch of things jump out and try to scare you. None of it is real. Relax and enjoy the ride," he said. Sara and I wanted to believe him.

The first thing we saw was a headless woman sitting in a rocking chair. Her head was in her lap and it was talking to us. "Turn back now. Go no farther, or you may never come out of here again."

"I think that we should believe what she is saying and leave," I said.

"Would you leave Sammy?" Brent asked.

"No. You're right, we have to find him. But I hope we can do it fast," I answered, just as the headless woman receded into the darkness.

The car turned a corner and came alongside a lumberjack dressed in a red plaid shirt, stocking cap, and jeans. He flashed a giant smile and raised his ax.

"I don't like the looks of this," I said.

Brent tried to assure me. "Haven't you ever seen one of those before? It's a robot. He'll lower the ax in a minute."

And he did.

He lowered it quickly and let go of it. The handle and glistening ax head flew our way. We dove for the floor of the amusement car. I heard the ax smash into the front of the car with a loud bang.

I was afraid to look, but I raised my head just slightly and peeked outside the car.

The lumberjack was gone. I looked at the front of the amusement car, and the ax was gone, too. There was no sign of either one anywhere.

"It's all right. The lumberjack is gone and his ax never really hit us," I said, exhaling a sigh of relief.

Sara popped up and looked at me. "What happened?" she said.

Before I could reply, Brent spoke up. "It was weird, and we are in the Tunnel of the Weird."

Sara's mouth fell open and she spit out the words, "Weirdness ahead!"

Brent and I turned to see our amusement car heading directly for a spinning buzz saw. "Jump out of the car," I screamed.

"That's crazy. There is nothing but wall on both sides of us. We are doomed!" Sara said, panic rising in her voice.

In another minute we would be doing more than panicking. In another minute we would be going to pieces—literally.

"We need to move to the sides of the car and let the blade pass down the middle," I yelled to the others.

Sara and Brent jumped to the left side of the car and I went for the right.

The car moved closer and closer to the blade. The sound got louder.

We were about a foot from the blade. I could feel the breeze from the fast-turning toothed wheel. I prayed that we would survive the cut.

Then we were about six inches away. Suddenly the car shifted and my body faced the blade.

This was the end for me.

"Help!" I screamed. As I did that the amusement car leaped forward, pulling us out of the way of the whirling blade.

"That was close," Sara cried.

"Way close," I agreed.

Brent sat back on the amusement car seat and spoke. "We came in here to save Sammy, and it looks like we may not make it out of here."

"Yes, we will," I said, trying to banish Brent's fears, although I wasn't convinced myself that we would make it out of the Tunnel of the Weird alive. "We'll find Sammy and get out of this place."

"Can we quit talking about finding Sammy and just find him? I want to get out of here as quickly as possible," Sara added.

Her statement was almost drowned out by the sound of rushing water. We looked at each other and then at what was ahead of us.

Our amusement car had gone into a flowing stream

of water that ran through the tunnel. And that stream headed straight for a waterfall. We couldn't tell how far down it was, but the crashing water sounds at the bottom were loud and violent.

"Hang on!" Sara yelled to make sure her voice sounded out above the water.

We all gripped the bar in front of us. I looked over at Brent. His eyes were closed and his lips were moving. I think he was praying. Sara was praying out loud.

We hit the edge and tipped forward.

Down and down the car fell.

The air rushed by us faster and faster.

We anticipated the crash, but it seemed like it was never going to come.

"I don't think that we are going to come out of this one. I'm really sorry for inviting you out here to my uncle's house. I wanted us to have fun, but instead it seems like we end everything right here," I apologized as we dropped through the rushing water.

Brent opened his mouth to say something when the car blasted into a pool of water and came to a dead stop, tossing us forward against the crash bar. It saved us from flying out and into the water. None of us were hurt.

"Wow!" Sara exclaimed. "I wonder what we're in for next?"

I looked at Brent. His face was greenish and he

looked very ill. "I'm not feeling too good," he said. "All this excitement is making my stomach tie in knots."

Sara didn't hear what he said. Her eyes were fixed on the object in front of us. Before us was the front of a castle. The turrets were built from large stones.

I wondered how the carnival workers built the large stone towers overnight. I needed to remember to ask Dr. Shivers when we got out of there. *If* we got out of there.

Our little ride car was heading straight for the big wooden door. It was a drawbridge, but it had not been let down yet. After the other weird things we had encountered in this tunnel I fully expected it to lower and take us inside. I was right.

The drawbridge eased down as we got closer. By the time our car got to the moat, the bridge was all the way down. We crossed it.

Not one of us said a word. Our silence told me that each of us was frightened about what we would encounter next.

We entered the castle. It was so dark inside that we could not see a thing. I heard the drawbridge rise again and close tightly behind us. We were not going to go back that way. We had no choice but to press ahead. Then the amusement car stopped. Sara sucked in a breath. Brent let out his breath, and I felt thankful to still have mine running through my lungs.

"What's next?" Brent asked.

"We have to stay calm. None of us know what we

are going to face next." I had barely finished saying that when we heard the sound of several feet stomping toward us in the dark. It sounded like they were wearing some type of armor.

The clanking metal grew louder, and we knew our welcoming committee was almost on us.

Sara yelled, "Run for it!" I felt her body leap from the car and then I heard a crash against metal. "Let me go!" Sara yelled.

# 26

"Sara, are you all right?" Brent called out into the darkness. I felt hands brush by me and Brent yelped and began to struggle. Then two strong hands grabbed me under my arms and another pair took hold of my legs.

We had been captured.

"Where are you taking us?" I demanded. No answer, only the sound of our captors' grunts.

Sara's voice and Brent's were not too far from me. The captors carried the three of us off in the dark. I had no idea where we were going, and I was afraid of where it could be.

Even though it was too dark to see, I could sense that we were placed inside a room. Brent breathed heavily and Sara whispered a prayer. But I was sure that there was another person in the room with us.

"Who is there?" I questioned.

"Me," a voice said.

"Sammy!" the three of us yelled in unison.

"We are really glad to see you," I said. "That is if we could really see you. How did you get in here?"

"I'm not sure. When the three of you went over to get balloons, I saw one of those hot dog stands and I wanted to get a barking hot dog for my little brother. When I got closer to the hot dog stand, one of the carnival workers invited me to try a new ride called the Well of Doom.

"I guess I'm a real sucker. I sat down in a bucket, and suddenly a dozen crazy things happened to me. To make a really weird story short, I ended up here," he told us.

"That isn't much different from what we experienced. We need to find a way out of here. Any ideas?" Sara asked.

"Have you found the walls or a door yet?" I asked.

"No, I just got here a few seconds before you did. It is too dark to see anything," he answered.

"I have an idea," Brent said with excitement.

"Spit it out," Sara said. "Anything would be helpful right now."

"We need to find a wall, but we don't know where the closest one is. I have a way to find it," he said. "I have some of that glow-in-the-dark putty that comes in an egg in my pocket.

"We can roll it up into a ball that we can throw against the walls. When it hits, it will bounce back like a rubber ball. Then we head to the closest wall," he told us with pride.

"That is the best idea I've heard in the last five minutes. I say we go for it," I encouraged.

The next thing I knew Brent was throwing the putty ball in the four directions around us. The first one took a while to come back. The second and third throws returned faster. The fourth one told us that we were only three feet from a wall.

Sara got to the wall first and pushed on it. Brent felt around for an opening. Sammy got frustrated and kicked the wall.

I was about to tell him not to lose his temper, when the wall gave a cracking sound. He kicked again. Something popped open.

"It's the door!" Brent screamed.

"Pure luck," Sara told Sammy.

"What do you mean? I knew exactly what I was doing," he joked.

"Instead of all this talk, I think we should get out of here before something else happens," I warned them.

We stepped through the doorway and stopped. We had stepped into what looked like a beautiful field. Bright lights shone above us, and what looked like green grass covered the ground.

I looked behind us. The door we came through was in the side of a wall. The number sixteen was painted on it.

"Where are we?" Brent asked with bewilderment.

"It looks like a big green field," I told him as I walked forward and looked around for a clue. "It doesn't look familiar, but we must be outside the carnival. Let's find our way back to my uncle's."

I raised my foot to take another step, but something grabbed me by the belt and hurled me to the ground.

**27**

"Why did you do that, Sammy?" I lay on my back on the ground and stared up at him.

"Hey, Bozo, you better watch where you are walking. You almost fell into a big hole in the middle of this green plastic field," Sammy said with a big laugh.

"A big hole in the middle of a green plastic field. It sounds like a miniature golf course to me. But that's silly. Everything on a miniature golf course is miniature," I said.

"Unless it is a giant miniature golf course," Sara interrupted.

I pulled myself up from the artificial grass and responded to Sara. "Why would you say that?"

"I didn't say that. The sign over there said it. I can't believe that we didn't see it before. It could have run us over, we were so close to it," she added.

"The sign may not run us over but there is a good chance that the big orange ball rolling toward us could," Brent said quickly.

"Golf course!" Sammy yelled.

"Big ball!" Sara screamed.

"Jump in the hole everyone," I commanded.

The other three went in before me. The hole did not have a flat bottom. This was one of the miniature golf course holes that sat on an upper deck. A bent tube connected the upper hole with the lower platform.

We needed to get to the bottom of the tube before the ball rolling at us dropped into the hole. That was what we needed to do, but that wasn't what happened.

Only seconds after I jumped inside the hole the ball fell in. Our giant must have been an awfully good golfer. We all slid down the tube with the ball behind us. It gained inches at a time. If it hit us we would be crushed inside the tube.

My mind was questioning how giants could exist and why they would have a miniature golf course. I didn't have time to come to any conclusions because the ball was gaining on us.

If I did not think of something quick, not much of us would be left to come to conclusions with.

Up ahead the tube split into two different ones. To avoid getting crushed, we needed to go down one and the ball needed to go down another

I yelled to the others, "Go down the left tube!"

Sara shifted her body and angled down the left side. Sammy and Brent followed. The ball was only a foot from my head. I had to take a gamble and go to the left.

If the ball came after me that would be the end of the game.

I slid feetfirst into the left tube and pushed off the side to give myself more speed so my head would clear the split before the ball bounced off my skull.

The golf ball nailed the divider and bounced to the side. I prayed that it would choose the right side. I prayed hard.

I looked back over my head. Was it going to follow me? Was this the final amusement for me at Dr. Shivers' Carnival of Terror? I closed my eyes and kept sliding downward.

After a few seconds, I opened my eyes again and looked back. The ball was gone. It went down the right tube. In another moment I popped out the bottom and fell onto the artificial grass.

"How did you know that we needed to take the left one?" Brent asked me excitedly.

"I'll tell you once we are out of this golf green. As long as we are in here the ball can get us any time. I don't feel like repeating that last experience. Jump the wall and then we will talk," I answered.

The four of us scrambled over the side and landed in another green.

"It looks like this is taking another bad turn," Sara whispered.

I agreed with her. "Sara, you're right. If we get out of this one, then I'm heading straight for the front gate and back to my uncle's pool. I have decided that I don't need any more excitement in my life."

"Actually, things are looking up," Sammy assured us.

"How?" asked Sara.

"There's a number seventeen painted on this wall. That means we only have to get through this green and the next one before we are done and out of here," he informed us.

"Great, but I still want to know how Kyle knew that we should take the left tube," Brent insisted.

"It was easy. My dad and I play miniature golf all the time. Any time there is a split tube, the builders put in a slight bump to send the ball down the side farthest from the hole.

"I could see that the hole was at the end of the left side. I assumed the ball would bounce down the right side."

"It saved us, Kyle. Thanks," Sammy added.

"Does anyone know where we should go next?" Brent quizzed.

"If we find the hole, then we find the place that will lead us to the next hole. What kind of hole is this?" I wanted to know.

"To get to the hole we have to go through there." Sara pointed to several large objects that were swinging back and forth. In their enlarged size, I was not sure what they were.

I guessed the swinging objects were large golf clubs. As we got closer it was easier to see them.

"What do we have to do, Kyle?" Sara said, placing her hand on my shoulder.

"Avoid the next ball," Sammy called to us as he bolted from our spot toward the center of the miniature golf fairway.

We turned our heads and saw another golf ball rolling toward us.

# 28

We leaped in step behind Sammy, running toward the clubs. The four of us had little choice. To make it to the clubs meant we probably would not get hit by the ball.

But the clubs were swinging back and forth in such a motion that we had to time it perfectly. And we did not even have time to think, let alone plan our run. This time it was either the clubs or the ball.

Sara reached the clubs first. She was the most athletic one of the bunch of us. She dodged and weaved. The first one missed her by only an inch. She let out a muffled scream.

She knew it was too close, but she could not turn back now.

The second one nipped her back heel. For a second she lost her balance. The delay worked in her favor. The third one went by easily. The fourth one was not destined to be so easy. I noticed that it moved at a faster rate of speed.

"Dive for it, Sara!" Sammy yelled. He must have noticed the rate of speed increase as well.

Without hesitating, Sara did as she was told and leaped forward like she was sliding into second base. It was a perfect base-stealing move.

Sammy faced the run next. I prayed that he would be as attentive to his own run as he had been to Sara's. He ran the first and stopped dead in his tracks and waited for the second to pass him.

It worked.

Brent watched Sammy and the two of them made it through.

I was glad that they made it, but I forgot to watch out for my own run. The first club narrowly missed me, but the second one was improperly timed.

It caught me and picked me up in the air. Its rate of speed propelled me into the air even farther. I was flying.

The air rushed through my hair and I felt gravity pulling at the skin of my face.

I looked down and saw the other three watching me with their mouths open. I felt more like a bird than a boy.

The club threw me up and over the wall. I started my fall back to earth and then realized that the artificial grass on the other side of the wall was very near. That saved me from broken bones and maybe even worse when I hit the grass. I had not fallen far enough to pick up much momentum.

"Kyle, are you all right?" Brent yelled up to me.

"I'm fine. You have got to get up here before the ball makes it through the clubs. I can see that the giant missed once, so he is going to try it again," I told them.

There was only one way and we all knew it. They would have to catch a club and let it throw them over the wall.

The giant's ball already was slicing through the barriers and would soon be rolling where they were standing.

The giant's ball bounced and hit the back wall. The ball rolled within a few feet of my friends.

"You've got to hitch a ride on one of the clubs and get up here before the next bounce nails you," I bellowed down to them.

My friends ran toward the clubs. The ball's bounce rolled it even closer this time. The next one would get them for sure.

Sara leaped first. It was the perfect jump. She grabbed on with her hands and swung off the club as it reached the high point. She dropped down next to me.

Brent was caught by the club and flew much like I did to the top of the wall. He fell with more impact, and I heard his breath rush out of him. The only one left was Sammy.

He followed Sara's lead and grabbed on. His body flew off the club with great momentum, and the sound of him hitting the ground was loud.

He didn't move at first. He opened his eyes slowly. "I don't feel very good. Can we just go home now?" Sammy asked in a whisper.

"More than gladly, but first we have to get out of here," Sara said.

"What do we do now?" Brent asked.

I stood up and pointed to the next green. "If I am right, that should be the eighteenth hole and we are out of here. I suggest that we—"

"That we what?"

My heart beat wildly.

"Get out of here fast before it gets us," I yelled.

## 29

My friends spun around. Coming toward us was something that looked like a gigantic mouth.

"What is it?" Sara gasped.

"I don't know. As long as it doesn't get any closer we can make it out of here," I said.

"When has anything stayed away from us? I don't think that we have much choice. We need to find a way through and out of the eighteenth hole. Let's run for it!" Brent said.

As the open mouth moved toward us I heard a loud hum coming from it. That's when I realized what it was—the nozzle of a vacuum cleaner. If we got too close we would be sucked inside a vacuum cleaner bag.

"Run faster. It's a vacuum cleaner. It will suck us up if we don't get to the next hole quick," I told them.

We reached the wall around the eighteenth tee. We didn't even think about what was on the other side.

We jumped into the air, grabbed the top of the wall, and vaulted over it. I could hear the vacuum go by us.

"We're safe," I said. But I spoke too soon. The eighteenth hole was surrounded by a high wall. We had expected that there would be a way out once we got there.

We were wrong.

"Well, I don't believe we are as safe as we thought. In fact, I don't believe that there is a way out of here," Brent said.

"We need to think of something quick. The ball will be rolling down on us any second. What is this hole like?" Sara said, taking charge of our situation.

I ran toward the hole and skidded to a stop. I had seen one of these before at Cascade Park Miniature Golf. It was the most difficult hole ever. The ball had to roll into a cup at the exact time that a powerful blast of air shot out of the cup. The ball would be pushed into the air before it dropped into the hole.

I explained to the others what we had to do. Everyone understood except Sammy.

"So we get in the hole, then what?"

"The last hole is not a cup. It is another tube that leads somewhere," I explained.

"Leads where?" Sammy asked.

"Out. I hope," I told him. Hoping was the best thing I could do.

We had only three choices. We could stay and risk getting crushed by a giant golf ball or we could jump over the wall again and risk getting sucked up by a vacuum cleaner. Our third choice, getting into the last hole, provided the best chance to escape.

"Brent you go first. Sammy, you go second, and Sara, since you are the fastest, you will need to go third. There won't be any time for mistakes by the time I go. Since I know the hole the best, I'll go last. Let's get moving before a ball heads our way," I instructed them.

"Too late, Kyle. The ball *is* heading our way," Sammy said.

Before Sammy finished his statement, Brent headed for the cup and the blast of air. He leaped in the cup and the air blasted him upward. He dropped into the hole and was out of sight.

Sammy was in the cup before Brent reached the hole. Sammy flew upward, but he twisted wrong and came back down into the cup. I turned around and saw the ball rolling closer to Sara and me.

"I don't think that you and I are going to make it before the ball arrives. Watch yourself as you run for the cup. Keep looking back because that ball is going to head for the hole as well."

I turned to look at Sammy. He was just dropping into the hole. That was two of us safe. Sara raced across the green. The ball was right behind her. She dove for the cup, and the blast of air shot her straight upward.

The ball was so close to her that the rushing air

pushed it backward. I was glad she beat the golf ball, but it was heading back toward me.

Sara dropped inside the hole. I was the only one left. The ball was rolling my way. There was something different about it. It was the color. It wasn't orange, it was white. If I was right, then there must be two players and I could expect a second ball in a few seconds.

My hunch was right.

As the orange ball rolled back toward me I felt the rumble of the white one moving up behind me. I was about to be sandwiched between the two golf balls.

I looked in front of me and then behind me. The two were about equal distance from me. I could not run fast enough to get away from the rolling menaces. An alternate maneuver was needed.

As the balls approached, I dove from between them. They hit each other, sending both golf balls in different directions. I lay on the artificial turf, watching them.

The orange one bounced off the wall and moved directly toward me. I rolled out of the way of the orange one.

This was a good short-term solution, but I needed a long-term one that would end up with me sliding down the eighteenth hole.

I jumped to my feet and started jamming my tennis shoes into the turf. I picked up speed, but so did the white ball. I hit the cup and was propelled into the air. I saw the hole that I needed to drop into below me. I twisted my body and down I went into the escape route.

I had made it out of the giant miniature golf course. I thought I was safe, but then the white ball dropped into the hole. It was rolling behind me in the tube. "Oh, no!" I shouted.

# 30

I could not believe that it was happening again. This time I did not have a split tube to save me. I was a good distance ahead of the ball as I approached the exit. That wasn't what worried me.

My stomach was in knots over what would happen when I dropped out and then the ball dropped out behind me. It would crush me.

I hit the exit and ran as fast as I could away from the end of the tube. I heard the golf ball drop out of the hole behind me. Still running, I turned my head to look behind me, but then I stumbled and crashed on the floor. The floor was spongy and prevented a painful smack.

I twisted my head to look at the golf ball. I wanted to see what would turn me into a pancake.

Before I could get a look at the ball, several hands grabbed me and yanked me away from the bottom of the tube. The golf ball bounced only an inch from my body and rolled into a bucket.

I looked up to see who had saved me. Sammy and Brent smiled back at me.

"We did it. We got out of there," I told them with relief showing across my face. "Where are we now?"

Sammy pointed to a door. "Sara went over to that door to see what was on the other side. She'll be back to tell us what is there in a minute. Just take a break and rest."

"I don't think we should do that. There is another golf ball that will be heading out of that hole in a second," I said.

We scrambled to our feet and ran for the door. Sara was waiting for us.

Sara smiled when she saw us. "I think this is all over," she yelled. "On the other side of this door is the nicest sight I've seen all day."

We opened the door and before us was a sign that said, TRANSYLVANIA TRAM TO DOCTOR SHIVERS' CARNIVAL OF TERROR. We were finally out of the Tunnel of the Weird and on our way home, or at least to the place that led to home.

"All aboard," said a voice from the speaker system above our heads. We slipped through the doors into a brand-new tram car. It looked more like a small subway car, but that didn't make any difference to us.

Our feet hurt and we were tired.

Brent stared at the walls around us. "Doesn't it seem strange that there isn't another person on this tram?" he asked.

"No, what's strange to me is that in one night Dr. Shivers could have set up a carnival and a tram system. I'm beginning to think that there is more to this place than we can see," I told them. "This Dr. Shivers does not have normal amusements in his carnival. It is more like something out of one of those horror books that all the kids at school are reading. I feel like we walked into the middle of one."

Brent looked very serious. "Do you think that we could have walked into one of those books? Is that possible?"

"Before we woke up this morning, I would have said that it was impossible. After everything I have seen, I have changed my mind," Sara said.

The tram slowed down and came to a stop. I looked out the window. It wasn't our stop. The sign read WEREVILLE. I thought that was a strange name for a town. "We have stopped at Wereville."

"Where- or were- or we're-ville. That is a really stupid name for a town. I wonder what it means? I wonder how a person is supposed to pronounce it?" Sammy added.

"Quiet. The door is opening. You will hurt the person's feelings who is getting on," Brent whispered to us.

A boy about our age slid through the open door. He smiled at us and said hello. We all returned his greeting. He sat down at the other end of the tram car.

Sammy continued his conversation. "What do they

say in Wereville? Do they say where is Wereville? Or do they say we are Wereville?"

"Or is it the werewolf of Wereville?" Sara joked.

"The werewolf of Wereville," I said thoughtfully. Then I said it again, "The werewolf of Wereville." After a moment or two, I said it again, "The werewolf of Wereville. That has a nice ring to it."

"Next you will be saying that the guy sitting down there is a werewolf," Brent said, chuckling.

# 31

We all laughed at Brent's joke and sat back in our seats. We were exhausted and needed to rest. Everyone was silent. The only sound was that of the tram moving over the tracks. The clickety-clack soothed me and I closed my eyes.

I was just about asleep when the tram slowed down again. I groggily asked, "Where are we?"

Brent put his face to the glass and looked outside. He turned around and told us that this stop was called Full Moon Junction.

"Werewolf of Wereville traveling through Full Moon Junction. Can this get any stranger?" I asked.

As I joked, the boy at the other end of the tram started to twitch and jerk. He held a hand up in the air. It was covered with hair. Then he leaped to his feet and growled. The boy twisted in the other direction and ran into the next car.

"What was that?" Sammy asked.

"It was really weird," Brent added.

"It was also a werewolf. He got on at Wereville, and then when we passed through Full Moon Junction the boy started to transform into a werewolf. Any minute now, he will walk through that door with only one thing on his mind," I explained.

"What?" Sara asked.

"Dinner. We are going to be his dinner," I expressed with unnatural calmness.

"Do you have any suggestions?" Sammy quizzed.

As he ended his question, the doors to the other tram car opened and the werewolf leaped through them.

"I have one suggestion, run!" I yelled loudly.

We all ran from our tram car to the next one. The werewolf didn't waste any time in ripping by the seats we had sat in. He smashed into the door and then through it.

We only had a few seconds to open the next door and leap through it into the tram car behind us. We repeated that process one more time as the werewolf jumped from seat to seat. He was tearing them up with his claws.

Sammy used his belt to tie the door handle to one of the metal bars used to steady standing people. It held for a few minutes.

The werewolf got madder and madder as he hit and pulled at the door.

"How many more tram cars do we have till we reach the end?" I asked.

126

Sammy pulled open the last door and looked inside. When he turned around, his eyes were filled with real fright. "The next car is the last one, and it is filled with all kinds of boxes and junk. There will be no place to run after that one."

"Great!" Sara said.

"What do you mean great? We could be dinner for a werewolf and you say that's great." Sammy was getting more animated as he spoke. His arms were flying in the air and his eyes were bugging out.

"I don't want to get eaten. I just want out of here."

The belt holding out the werewolf was stretching. The leather showed signs of splitting. I didn't think that we had more than another minute to move to the next car.

"Let's get into that other car. Once we are there we can find things to block the door," I called to my friends.

We yanked open the last door just as the werewolf ripped the leather belt. The werewolf's yellow eyes glared at us as he let out a tremendous howl.

Sammy, Sara, and I passed into the last tram car. After Brent entered, Sara slammed the door shut behind him, picked up a broom that lay on the floor of the car, and jammed it into the door to hold it shut. The werewolf smashed his face against the glass of the door. His hot breath steamed the window.

We backed against the variety of junk in the last car.

All of us started looking and scrambling through the boxes.

"I found something that might work," Brent yelled out as he pulled a chain from under a stack of rags.

He and Sammy ran to the door and wrapped the chain through the handle and around the bottom of a spare seat stored in the car.

"What do we lock it with, Brent?" Sammy asked.

"I don't know. What can we lock it with, Kyle?"

I found a small rope. I looked at it and then looked back at the chain. It could work, but then the chain could still break. We didn't have a lot of choices. I tossed it to Brent. "Try this. It won't hold for long, but it will keep him out while we try to figure out something else."

Brent and Sammy tied the chain together with the rope and wrapped it as tightly as they could.

The werewolf continued to smash his body against the glass of the door. His howls were getting louder.

I glanced around at my friends. Fear strained their faces as they wildly tore through the boxes of junk, looking for something to use for protection. Fear controlled us and we were reacting out of panic. I needed to say something to calm down everyone.

"Hey, we have been in some pretty tight spots in Dr. Shivers' carnival, and each one turned out all right. What are we so worried about? The werewolf could change back any minute or turn around and run off the tram."

Sara stared at me. "This is a tram heading to the carnival. I don't think the same rules apply to this game as in all the others. Our best bet is to keep him out of here."

The tension was getting to us all. I had to do something to get rid of this werewolf and save my friends. I climbed down off the stack of boxes and spotted a shovel. I picked it up and walked toward the door.

Sammy stepped in between the door that held back the werewolf and me. "What are you doing?" he asked.

"I'm going to get us out of this predicament. When I open the door and smash the werewolf with the shovel, all of you jump out the back door. Run as fast as you can, and I will hold him off as long as I can." My voice quivered with fear as I spoke.

One of us had to stop him, and it was going to be me. I pushed Sammy out of the way and took a few more steps toward the door.

Suddenly the tram lurched forward, then backward. I did not have to walk the last few steps to the door. The tram tossed me toward the door, and I hit it with a heavy thud.

The werewolf was less than an inch away.

**32**

The werewolf was pressed against the other side of the window. His fierce eyes glowered at me.

The tram had come to a complete stop. The werewolf backed up. I thought he was getting ready to run right through the door.

I bent down and picked up my shovel. He was not going to get through me.

When I stood up again, he was gone. I thought he might be hiding. I waited. The werewolf could attack again, and I wanted to be ready for him.

"Look!" Brent screamed with excitement. "The werewolf got off at this stop. We are safe."

"Where are we?" Sara asked.

Sammy looked at the nearest sign. "This is the stop for Monster Middle School. Why would he be out of school at this time of the day?"

"He went out for lunch. We were going to be his fast food. 'I'll take four kids, please, and hold the mustard,'" Sammy blurted out.

I started laughing. Then Sara picked it up, then Brent. We kept laughing until the tram began moving again. As we pulled away from the Monster Middle School, a voice came over the speaker above us.

"Last stop coming up, Dr. Shivers' Carnival of Terror. We hope you enjoyed your ride. Please ride the Transylvania Tram again soon."

"Finally, we are back at the carnival. I never thought that I would be glad to be back at the Carnival of Terror," Sara said. We all agreed as we sat motionless, waiting to see the carnival up ahead. The tram came to a slow and easy stop. The door opened and we entered an enclosed area.

The four of us stumbled into the sunlight and out into the midway. Nobody said anything. We started to run toward the gate. As we turned the corner to leave, we saw the clown and several others walking toward us.

Something was different about the clown. He had taken off his makeup. I recognized him. I couldn't believe who it was.

It was my Uncle Rex. Behind him were several men and women with clipboards and communication headsets. In our confusion we ran up to him.

"Uncle Rex, you've got to have this place closed down. It's too frightening. Kids will be scared to death here. Dr. Shivers has monsters that tried to eat us and rides that tried to kill us. He even has giants that play miniature golf." The words tumbled out of my mouth.

Finally, it hit me—Uncle Rex was wearing the clown suit. I saw it before, but my joy of seeing him overrode my realization that it was the same clown outfit. I was puzzled.

"Uncle Rex, why are you dressed like a clown?"

Then I heard a gruesome laugh come from behind me. I spun around and saw Dr. Shivers. He looked different as well. His hat was off and his goatee was gone.

Brent gasped.

Uncle Rex looked at me. "Great! You kids were great."

We must have given him the most puzzled looks he ever saw. He started to laugh. "Kids, I wanted you all to come to this carnival."

"Why? Did my dad do something to you when you were a kid and now you're paying me back for it?" I asked.

"No, this is the set for my new TV series called, of course, 'Dr. Shivers' Carnival of Terror.' I wanted to test the planned frightening amusements on kids who didn't and couldn't know anything about it. So I called your dad and told him what I had planned. We wanted four kids from the Midwest to come out here and be our guinea pigs. You four were fantastic."

Sara's face broke into a big smile. "Then everything we saw was made by illusions and special effects?"

"Exactly," Uncle Rex answered.

"Then I never ate any worms?" Brent said with relief.

"Nope, it was real cotton candy with a hologram inside it. Pretty neat, huh?" my uncle responded. "Now, I want you to meet Dr. Shivers. I'm sure you recognize him. This is Johnny Tate."

Brent looked at him with a smug smile. "I knew you looked familiar," he said, giving Johnny an I-knew-it-all-along look. Johnny Tate was the famous teen television star.

"The good news, kids, is that we filmed all the things you did. Some of the stuff that went wrong, like the splinter from the small explosions in the Gremlins' Gallery, will have to be fixed, but mostly we wanted to see how you reacted. We'll use those scenes for the opening credits of the TV show. And better yet, you'll all get paid for it," my uncle rattled on.

Sammy jumped in front of me. "Do you mean we'll be on TV every week? I'll be a star?"

"Kind of, Sammy. In fact you gave us some of our best footage. After we take it back to the studio and make the edits and cuts, I'll bring it home for you all to see.

"Now, I need to get my crew together to close things down. Why don't all of you head back to the house and we'll have dinner together," Uncle Rex said.

"Will Johnny be coming?" Sara asked.

"I wouldn't have it any other way," Uncle Rex responded.

We had started back to the gate when my uncle called, "Hey, Sammy, catch."

Through the air came the barking hot dog. Sammy caught it and we all laughed. He got his souvenir of Dr. Shivers' Carnival of Terror after all.

As we walked back to the house, Sammy nudged me and said, "Nothing like this back in our little town."

The dream was too real. I was afraid to open my eyes. I feared that a large black spider was hovering over me with its mouth wide open. I had no desire to face the same fate as a careless fly. But I had to look. I had to know what was going on. I forced an eye open. Then a second one. I couldn't believe what I was seeing.

The electric blanket was rolled around me like a cocoon. It squeezed me. It was all I could do to scream out to my brother, "Jonny, get in here. Your joke is not funny. Get me out of this right now!"

There was no response from Jonny. I heard him playing a video game in his room. The sound was loud, and he was yelling. I yelled to him three more times. No answer. I had to figure a way out. But how in the world did an ordinary electric blanket wrap itself around me? Before I could figure that out, my electric blanket squeezed me again. I yelled for Jonny. I was beginning to think that this wasn't one of his little pranks.

The blanket was getting hotter. The sweat dripped down my face. If I didn't get out of it soon, I would be cooked. I had no plan, and I had few opportunities. The blanket tightened.

I had to unplug the blanket. It worked for the hair dryer. The hair dryer that had nearly taken my life a few minutes ago seemed to have been an easy challenge compared to the blanket. I had to think of a way to unplug the cotton hot plate.

I started to rock my body back and forth. I moved only an inch or two. I didn't have a lot of confidence that rocking was going to work. I rocked again. Nothing. I rocked harder back and forth, and after ten rocks, I finally rolled over. Unfortunately it was the wrong way. I got closer to the plug and not farther away.

I didn't have much of a choice. I had to call for Jonny again. The noises were very loud in his room. I could hear him screaming and yelling at his video game. I had never known him to get into a game like that before. I was sure he wouldn't hear me, but I tried screaming one more time. I was right. Jonny didn't call to me or run into my room. I would have to find my own way out of this mess.

I was trying to roll again when my brother ran into the room.

"Anna, you have to see this," he yelled. Then he stopped at the foot of my bed. "What are you doing? Why are you wrapped up in the blanket like that? Are you cold or something?"

"Listen, you little twerp, I know you did this to me while I was asleep. I want you to let me out of this now. Unwrap me or I'll stomp on your computer chips," I cried out to him.

"I didn't do it. I was in my room playing with this really weird new game I discovered. You've got to see it," he said excitedly.

"I'd like to, but I seem to be all wrapped up in my work here. Maybe I'll stop by after I break free," I joked. I hoped my brother would understand that I was in a serious situation. I needed his help. "Listen, Jonny, I'm sorry. It probably wasn't you, but I can't figure out what is going on around here. A few minutes ago my hair dryer attacked me, and now my electric blanket is trying to do me in. So would you please do something here?"

"What? 'I'm a doctor, Jim, not an electrician,'" he quoted in his best Dr. McCoy from *Star Trek* voice.

The blanket squeezed tighter. I had to get out of it soon. I said to my brother, "When the hair dryer attacked me, all I had to do was unplug it. I hope that is all we have to do now. So walk over there and unplug this thing."

"Where is the plug?"

I sighed. "It's under the bed."

"You expect me to crawl under your bed and unplug the blanket? Do you know how dirty it is under there? Forget it!" he said.

"Jonny, I'm going to tie the tails of your computer mice together."

"Anna, I'm kidding you. I'll let you out of this if you come with me and see what is going on in my room. Is it a deal?" Jonny was driving a hard bargain.

"Deal. Now let me out, please," I begged.

Jonny reached under my bed and unplugged the blanket. It unwound and I was free.

"Okay, now you've got to see what's going on in my room," he said. He pulled me off my bed. I followed him out of my room to his.

He chattered the whole way there. "I don't know what's causing it, but do you know that video game *Gunslinger*? It's really acting up. I'm supposed to be able to fire the electronic impulse gun at the gunslingers and score points—"

"So what's wrong?" I interrupted.

"Well, they keep firing back at me," he said.

"What do you mean?" I asked as we turned the corner into his room. The moment we stepped inside, something hit Jonny's piggy bank and it exploded, raining pennies, nickels, and dimes all over the place. I looked at the video screen. A gunslinger was aiming at us again. I jumped on top of Jonny, and we went tumbling to the floor as another shot struck just above us on the shelf. One of Jonny's books hit the ground. The whole thing gave me goose bumps.

Twelve-year-old Anna and ten-year-old
Johnny look forward to a quiet day at home
while their parents work, but they soon find
themselves scrambling for cover when their
home-sweet-home takes on a life of its own.

It's too late to leave home in . . .

# Attack of the Killer House

## SpineChillers™ #2
### by Fred E. Katz